South Side of Sanity

By

Shane Hoffman

Avid Readers Publishing Group
Lakewood, California

South Side of Sanity

Avid Readers Publishing Group

http://www.avidreaderspg.com

ISBN-13: 978-1-935105-62-6

Printed in the United States

Chapter 1
Two Sides of the Coin

June 27th, the day that I would leave to spend the week in San Diego, California would be one to fill most people's memories for their life but it was just a step in what would be a future of misunderstandings and people for me.

Finally done with high school, it was time to celebrate freedom from what was known as a death trap of days that ran together like episodes of Sex and the City. The catch was to spend it with the only girl you have lived to satisfy since you started to grow pubic hair on your crotch and her homosexual brother and his newfound black man. What I would find out was hard was not the one week stay in San Diego, but the two day an twenty two hour drive that it took to get there.

After promising my mother and father that may stay in California would be filled with site seeing and praising hotel singers, I left to the nearest liquor store to buy a big bottle of Jack Daniels not the little one the big one, and a case of cold, cold Heineken; a quote from Kix that I was fond of. Pedro, Juan, or Enrique it doesn't matter was working the store and getting a fake identification card past them would end up being the second easiest thing I ever did.

Upon arriving to my house to pick me up, Leah the only girl that I had ever spent any time with texted me to make me promise her that I wouldn't have any smart ass remarks for her brother and his new man. Thinking of all the insensitive comments that I could possibly use I decided to be mature for once in my life and keep my mouth shut.

Giving my hellos to everyone as I climbed into the vehicle I looked at Leah with the reality that we were actually over with. She was this girl of average height, long brown curly hair, and a birthmark on her forehead where she used her hair to cover. Her eyes were large and beautiful and my best guess told me they were brown also. Leah's best trait was her smile because it had this way of making me feel good no matter how terrible I felt, but what I loved most was how she was always willing to fuck me no matter how unattractive I could and would be at times.

Her brother was also one of my best friends and it didn't matter to me whatsoever what it took to float his boat, as long as the boat wasn't floating towards me. I most respected him because he consistently looked out for his younger sister and took shit from no one. Especially the people in school who tried to make fun of him but stopped once they had realized he was a trained boxer who could fuck anyone up if he so pleased.

Unfortunately for me, Leah and I didn't speak a word to each other during that long exhausting trip. And every time I found myself nodding off to sleep I would end up dreaming of our times together.

Unlike most girls that spent their high school years in the 21st century Leah enjoyed the same style of music as me and was always willing just to hang out and not be a total fucking drama queen. That was until I found her having sex with the temporary Spanish teacher who had just arrived from Puerto Rico. He was everything I wasn't during that year, smooth, sexy, and able to make any female scream with passion during sex. Leah thought that it wouldn't have mattered since it was with an older man, but anytime you are with a girl and she lets another man pleasure her, it's a sure sign of the end times with you and her.

It was as though that sting that I had felt from her would never go away, no matter how hard I tried.

2

Inside of me I knew that she did this just to break us up. Leah was having a rough time with both of us finally being done with high school and going to different colleges so she did what any other she wolf would have done and slept with another man. She was always telling me how my sense of adventure and spontaneity was lame and not up to her standards. Leah's adventurous side consisted of wanting to go skydiving, bungee jumping, and holding your breath under water just long enough to stay alive. My spontaneity was in the realms of having sex in the gay and lesbian section in a Barnes & Noble, knocking on neighbor's doors and running away, and pocketing as many candy bars as we possibly could in a local convenient store.

Granted, Leah was correct when she said I was just a child and my ideas were ridiculous but who the hell needs to jump out of an airplane to feel alive. I knew that her ideas were bullshit because she would never follow through with them unlike me. Just like any young kid who tries convincing others that they have this undying desire to set the world afire, she was just trying to fit in.

When I was in eighth grade I learned from Leah that when you decide to finger a girl that it's best you use more than one finger to excel the pleasure and to be accurate with the term. When I was in ninth grade I learned that eating out a girl meant placing your tongue in her valued part. Always feeling like a day late and a dollar short, Leah always managed to keep me on track.

We would spend our weekends hanging out at her place listening to her dad's old Poison albums. This was only because of the fascination she had with the lousy television show of the middle aged Bret Michaels. I guess he still could attract someone half of his age. Like I had mentioned, her taste in music differed greatly from girls of today's age. Even though I hated Poison because they were nothing but a full out chick band, I enjoyed listening to them with her because

3

it beat the weak shit sounds of Soulja Boy and All American Rejects. For her sixteenth birthday I learned the chords to Every Rose Has Its Thorn from that 1980's chick hair band and worked up the courage to play and sing it for her. It was quite simple, seeing how Bret Michaels was far from being a guitar god. Leah's father brushed off my gift as me being too cheap to actually go out and buy something that cost money. And he proceeded to run all of my values into the ground once more.

My once pimple covered puberty face was only loved by Leah and the fact that she wasn't impressed by the white punks who were wannabe black men and the preps who spent an hour in front of the mirror each morning trying to look like Nick Carter. She also never made any complaints to me when I told her that feeling inside of her vagina felt strange the first time. That would change in the months to come as I learned to crave it instead.

Up until Rico Suave had sex with my girl, I was the only one who knew that she went numb from her knees down when she had an orgasm.

Finally, we arrived at our destination and got unpacked into our hotel room and Leah's brother and his mate were gone for the night. Lying on the bed flipping through channels trying to find The King of Queens or Everybody Loves Raymond Leah finally came in and decided to speak to me for the first time since we had left. Sitting on the edge of the bed she had began to get all teary eyed and explain how sorry she was for breaking us up and that she desperately needed me to forgive her for her moment of weakness.

I couldn't take her back, finding her with another man was like finding out I was adopted or was never really loved by a hand that touched me. Still, she was persistent on making up with me, so before I had a chance to respond she jumped my bones and began humping me. Breathing up and down my neck and chest, her moans got louder and her hair was flying around like she was staring in a Poison music video. Ramming my dick in her as hard as I could it was only seconds later that I had managed to cum.

Knowing damn well that I just received a pity fuck, I took it to the fullest extent and did what I could to make her feel bad the rest of our stay there. The ride in the elevator to the bottom floor was awkward enough after our stint in the hotel room. We made our way into the local long john silvers where sitting down to eat would prove to be the most embarrassing meal and stay at a public outing. Leah wanting to continuously take things further managed to rub her foot on my just unloaded dick and make it hard again. Throwing it off several times, her hand now rubbing on me, once again made me cum, but this time it was in my pants and visible to everyone in the restaurant who was enjoying a cheap meal with their families.

Only after being spotted by the fifteen-year-old girl mopping up the bathroom floors did I know it was time for me to leave. If that wasn't bad enough the manager chased Leah and I out of the establishment. Laughing hysterically like she did when we first started seeing each other I batted a mean eye her way to let her know that I was anything but happy. Still trying to make things right, Leah suggested that I have sex with another girl to even the score. Not believing in myself at the moment in my cum stained pants, I left it up to her to find someone that would even our score. Leah like any female went out and got a girl that I couldn't fuck if I somehow managed to drink a whole bottle of Jack Daniels.

This once again led to another fight between Leah and I and one that would end any further conversation or fucking. Asking her to permanently stay out of my life, I tossed the television set out of the hotel and took all of her belongings and threw them out also. My voice was so loud that it warranted the people staying in the room next to us to call the police.

Leah's constant hysterical screaming and crying made police believe that I was abusing her and this led to a beating by one of the pigs. Only after my beating did she finally tell the police that I hadn't hurt her and everything was just a misunderstanding.

I would have preferred being taken away by the police because her brother came in only minutes after they left and gave me the biggest ass beating of my life. No pun intended. Spitting blood like it was saliva her brother and boyfriend continued to kick my ass and throw all of my shit out on the curb leaving me to fend for myself.

Taking my lonesome beat up self to the bar with my fake I.D. I began slamming shots like it was going out of style. Still wearing my Motley Crue Shout at the Devil shirt that Leah bought me when I was in tenth grade I began feeling like the main character in The Outlaws There Goes Another Love Song. Sitting there I was confronted with a Cuban woman that resembled the wife on The George Lopez show. She sat across the bar from me and kept making her eyes shift over to my side. Sucking on her straw in a very provocative way, she ordered me a drink. When it arrived the bartender told me the lady at the end of the bar sends her compliments. After this incident, I have learned that when a woman buys you a drink it's time to get out of there before you end up in my predicament.

The beautiful Cuban woman finally made her way over to me and asked what was keeping me down. Nothing but the usual daily struggles I said half-heartedly. Smiling she said in a hard to understand, yet sexy voice, well I know how those days go. The George Lopez wife look alike was starting to make it clear that she was willing to make my troubles go away for a while. The misunderstanding lies on my behalf because when you are born and raised in a Mid-West town, you forget that everywhere else in the world isn't like your backyard. The only difference between her and

Angie was she couldn't speak English very well and I latter found out that her underarms were hairy.

Feeling like my luck was starting to change because she bought me a few drinks and wanted me to unload my current frustrations on her. Eventually after being drunk off my ass and being vulnerable the nice Cuban woman led me into her vehicle and made my dick explode in ways I have only read about. Bouncing up and down on me, she smacked her head against the roof of the car and let out a painful fuck, a word she knew very well in English. Her nipples were large and almost made me suffocate. Her semi large thighs had me pinned down in the seat. Thinking that I was on my game she asked me for two hundred dollars. Puzzled I just looked at her with a smile hoping that she was only kidding around with me. She stared right into my eyes with a dark cold stare that could kill.

Unfortunately, this wound up being just another snap-shot of my vacation. Never believing that I would get my ass kicked by a pimp because I fucked a hooker and couldn't come up with the funds to cover the cost, it happened. Taking one kick in the ribs after another I felt like there wasn't any more blood to spit out but once again I was wrong. For the first time in my life I actually thought I was going to die. After taking on ass beating after another I blacked out.

Waking up in an alley it dawned upon me that I had no money and I got the shit beat out of me by a pig, queer, and pimp in one night. Still, I was set to enjoy the rest of my time there even if half of my funds were now gone and I didn't have a ride home.

Picking myself off the ground I walked my sore self to the beach and just took in all the sun and scenery that was surrounding me. The warmth felt great as I lied there and tried not to move too much because of my shattered ribs and jaw. Walking along the beach led to being the only thing I did for that day. During the night the water felt extra cool as I let it take me in an out to shore. The realization of my predicament didn't mean anything to me. I kept thinking about the situation with Leah and how shit went down between us.

My thoughts run rapid through the corridors of my mind and produce life long memories that soon become my only connection to the world and its heartbeat. The psyche-delic evening of Leah and I as we came one on one with out innermost beings. Flying through the quiet streets of our ghost town, we came tumbling down through fields and fields of open land. Clinging to each other as to find our brilliant youth and inexperience as a way to make it through the years that made us who we are or weren't.

Diving into each other's eyes as we search through the soul to free our innermost ambitions, Leah decides to breathe hard and let out a cry of desperation and dying hope. We both understand each other in a way only two mentally disturbed individuals could. There is a tear that is undeniably warm falling down her face and into her mouth. The heartbeat that was once strong and vibrant, now slow but hard. She jams her nose and mouth into my ear with a weak voice that follows.

The sky is lit up in a way only God could make it. The moon is brighter than the sunshine during a hot summer day. Everyone's current world is black and cloudy, making it impossible for him or her to see. Ours however is shining only through our deepest emotions and fears. Softly pushing my lips up to Leah's cheek, I quietly express my love like it is the only genuine creation to ever wander the lonely earth. Leah finally speaks telling me her parents are getting a divorce and she questions whether or not the split will dictate the rest of her life and separate us to a point of no return. I tell her in the surest voice I can gather that no matter what we would always be together.

I now know that in life there are no fairytales or miracles that make everything all right. We just make ourselves go through life desiring the best but accepting mediocrity. The human psyche is only designed to accept the average. Our dreams are our only source of escaping. They allow us to become whatever it is we want or run away from on a daily basis. The dreams are we at the core of our souls. They're the most honest things we know. My dreams are an extension of my mind and existence. The one thing that allows me the freedom to live and die. I die in them with vengeance that is only cured when the morning sun comes rising through my window and onto my eyes. Yea I guess it is a bet with my mind. Just games that I try desperately to win like a person being killed under false charges.

The last memory between us that I would keep for awhile was the first time we ever kissed. Or should I say the first time I ever kissed a girl.

Being thirteen in junior high meant finding your place and new self in the new school. We lived nine miles apart and everyday during that summer I would ride my skateboard over to her house to talk about all the teachers we hated and talked like children did about running away together and making it on our own without the help of our never understanding parents. Especially, since Leah's father was a pastor of some sort and didn't want his daughter anywhere nears a guy like me. He viewed me as a guy who was stuck in the wrong decade with the wrong hobbies and girlfriend. He even black balled his son once he found out about his sexual preferences.

Her back porch crouched down Leah and me and she quickly leaned in and kissed me, I couldn't even be man enough to initiate the kiss. Instead I enjoyed every second of it as she put her hand on my left cheek. Either it was my imagination or reality but the stars seemed to be shining extra bright and high in the sky.

Taking my liquor and booze as the only thing I could

offer anyone as I hitched hiked back home the next day. The different drivers that picked me up varied from truck drivers hitting on me to overage hippies in vans smoking crack to someone just wanting someone to talk to.

Finally arriving home actually felt like a relief. Not wanting to send my parents into a crisis mode I told them that the trip went as planned and how much I was looking forward to doing the same thing once I graduated college. Leah had sent me a text message that read

I won't forget you babe
Even though I could

A quote from her favorite Poison song that I hated with passion but once again liked just because it wasn't today's music.

I looked at that text message for the next few months but stopped once I was into my first month in college due to another woman who would find her way into my bed. Taking my best effort at a Poison song, I decided to send it along, as to say that we were finally done with one another. I was hoping Leah would take our first song written together and believe that it didn't mean anything to me anymore. This was just the beginning of my odyssey.

Moonlight

I dream of you when I'm sleeping
I can't describe this feeling
When I'm holding you in my arms so tight
Being so close during this movie tonight
God only knows it's so right
Your eyes shining in the moonlight

As we are walking home tonight
Tell me that you love me
While your holding me in your arms tight
Let me know its good, let me feel its right
Kissing the tenderness of your lips
When no ones in sight
While your eyes shine in the moonlight

Cause' when the seasons have changed
And I'm just a memory
I want you to know I loved you
In perfect harmony
Even sweeter than a melody

If you put your head on my shoulders
And your hands on my chest
I could rest easy knowing you were mine
And with a simple kiss
You'd understand I'm just a man out of time
And I'd write a few lines
Just to get that perfect rhyme

Let me love you
Like you never been loved before
Let me know your mine
As you close the door
And I pick the pieces of my heart
Off the floor
I Had a Dream I was in Love.

If you think I don't love you
Because my face never seems to smile
Don't believe it because it just isn't true
You're someone I couldn't live without even for awhile

If tears begin to form in your eyes
And your heart starts to break
Kiss the memories and their ties
Loving you could never be a mistake

Think of me every once in awhile
And be sure to always keep that innocent smile
That made the flowers bloom in your name
And kept me from going insane
In times of sorrow and desperate rain

My skies my be burdened with clouds
And my truths weighed down by lies
But I couldn't make it without your face in my mind
Our love were pieces scattered on the floor I just couldn't
find

That kiss was just once upon a time for me
Like the waves crashing on the shore
You know I faked my eyes being too blind to see
I made you think I didn't love you anymore

Somehow it'll all work out in some fashion or another
Sometimes it happens that she isn't my lover
Other times I've paved the way
For painful tears that come and stay

Bye bye baby I hate to leave
Knowing I'll never see you again
This feeling I surely can't let go
You may never understand and I may never know

Some say she's my only friend
With me until the end
No one knows

Just how her love flows
Right through me and fills my soul

I met her on a busy end street
She says she's never missed a beat
Children cry for her and men give up their seat
To appease her and the losing streak
That lives in her eyes and remains to be seen
Like a movie played out on the silver screen

The days have passed and the cracks are deeper
In the way you've always admired
If there's someone out there who knows her
Tell her my minds made my body grow tired

I had a dream I was in love
And she was the girl I was dreaming of
Still in the night whispering silent words
That chilled my body with meaning absurd

13

Chapter 2
Say What You Will

It's 3:23 in the morning and I'm lying in my bed staring at the ceiling. Everyone is sleeping and the entire house is silent. My thoughts are running rampant and I just can't seem to keep my eyes closed long enough to fall asleep.

Finally tired of lying there I decide to get up and go outside and just breathe in the summertime air. While I'm out there I find myself getting into my car and pulling out of the driveway. Cruising down the road I am going just under the speed limit and I'm taking in everything around me. The trees, houses, lawns, and signs that are surrounding me. I find that the faster I go the less I see and remember the scenery. With my foot on the pedal I continue to go faster and faster and soon I look at the speed dominator and I'm flying going at ninety-five miles per hour and even one hundred at times.

Soon everything around me is just a blur and my thoughts are racing at a million miles per hour and nothing is sinking in anymore. My body feels paralyzed except for my feet. My mind is lost in disarray and confusion and nothing seems to make sense. For some reason, I'm afraid to turn around in the vehicle for fear that someone or something is behind me getting ready to attack. It's as though I know my death is coming, but I rather have it sneak up on me rather than see it coming and feel all the effects from it.

In a way, all of this is just like life. The faster we go the faster we get to our death. We don't allow ourselves to appreciate all the beautiful things that surround us everyday. We are taking it all for granted and we keep going faster and faster and soon we are at our deaths and we are just left questioning everything we have ever been taught.

Wondering where did the time go? How did all of this come to be? Even, when we see disasters before us we decide to put on blinders in hope that the situation will just disappear and dissolve itself. Our mind starts playing nasty tricks on us and convincing us the less we feel the less we will be harmed. But, in hindsight we will end up feeling a lot more and the feelings won't be kind.

But just like when I was in the vehicle, the slower I went the more I got to take in. The chance to experience everything increases greatly and starts to develop our minds and thoughts into something we can understand and take comfort in. All of sudden our blood pressure decreases and slowly but steadily our body relaxes and we are at one with ourselves. The realization that life is short starts to take on a whole new meaning and it's a positive one because we are realizing it before we are too old to do anything about it. For some reason, life suddenly has a purpose and we aren't screaming all the time and our problems become simple solutions. But, be careful not to start living in fantasy because that's just as dangerous.

The time I spent in the vehicle slowly turns minutes into hours and the sun is just about to rise. Still going at a speed of one hundred miles per hour I see a figure in the rising fog but I'm not sure if it's a person standing there or an animal. As I'm slamming on the breaks the car starts to twist and turn out of control. Too late to stop, I realize the figure in the fog is a woman and in a blink of an eye I crash right into her. Right as I begin to hit the windshield I wake up.

Sweating profusely with a heartbeat that's going through the ceiling, I look over to my left and lying in bed next to me is a woman. I guess it would be appropriate to use that term loosely to describe her. She's someone that wouldn't know how to describe herself if her life depended on it.

She is just sitting there with that smile on her face that says she is proud of what she had done. The only thought running through my mind was how I got back to my room that night. Looking at me, this woman finally speaks asking if I would prefer her to go home, lying there desperately trying to gather my thoughts it takes everything for some reason for me to speak. After gathering all of my courage I tell her that it doesn't matter but she should think about leaving soon because I have to go to work in the next hour. Of course you do she says with a giggle, acting as though she had heard it all before. She starts to gather her belongings while telling me that she has a lot of homework to catch up on and then she herself has to head to work.

Glancing over again to me she says you know I could end up being the love of your life. You just never know how things will work out; maybe we'll end up in each other's arms just like a Disney fairytale would have it. Knowing that she is only trying to play games with my mind I respond with a smile that's trying to guide her out the door but like any girl that I have had the pleasure or displeasure to know, she doesn't know when to take a hint and if she does the girl just doesn't care.

Where would I be if I lost this dark side of me? I decide to give her something else to think about with my latest comment. Why must you always be so gloom and looking on the dark side of life, she asks? Nothing is ever as bad as you make it out to be. Or maybe nothing is as good as everyone makes it out to be, I quickly snap back. Coming over just one last time to give me a kiss on the cheek, she finally leaves.

She has this sway to her walk that reminds me of a movie star with broken confidence, she moves in a way that makes me want to grab her and fuck her again but I know that I am pushing my luck to the extreme with her. If I take things any further I could end up doing time in the slammer, and that's the last thing that I want for my future time and reputation. Not that I have much of either of them but the little I have managed to secure I'd like to keep. Watching her leave, makes me question whether or not I should have asked her to go and instead got a quickie out of the way instead of taking care of it in the shower.

As she finally leaves my room I just sit up in bed and think how nice it was to end my four-month drought of any female companionship, though in the back of my mind I'm constantly asking myself if it was truly worth it. Regardless, I grab my portable cd player because I have yet to gather the money for an iPod and I pop in John Cougar's first disc and immediately skip to my favorite song Do You Think That's Fair then right to Sugar Marie. Slipping slowly away I take a quick half hour nap before I need to get up and head back to school for the week. But not before I have my usual thoughts on the world because it helps ease my own guilt of wrongdoing.

I think that women will purposely hurt you to satisfy themselves in anyway they see fit. Even, if doing what they are doing to hurt you really hurts them twice as bad. Women who are essentially not from the same planet as men are so wired different that they themselves never know if they are coming or going most of the time. They will to no end hurt themselves until they are sitting in some psychiatrist's office paying him an ungodly amount of money for him or her to tell them what they already know.

Unfortunately, for men the woman will go to a woman doctor and be brainwashed into thinking that all of their pain and suffering comes from how women have been treated by men since the beginning of time. Never mind that most of the men around today weren't around since the beginning of time. The extreme feminists around for the most part have ruined society with all of their ridiculous ways. In reality, back in the day if I can call it that a lot of the women who were living those "roles" were satisfied with the way things were.

You always got that one guy in the crowd that supports every lame ass thing a woman does because he wants a piece of ass more than he wants his own sanity back. And anyone who opposes these views is a male chauvinistic pig. This is complete bullshit because that would make me one, when in fact I'm one of the biggest supporters of women. I love them all.

The world without a doubt is at our fingertips. We slowly but steadily craft our children's minds into hateful envious bastards. Hate, unfortunately today is a family value. Nobody anymore has an original thought left in his or her god-forsaken brain. Everything is just recycled all the time. I feel like we are walking breathing viruses.

Also, wouldn't it be logical for all of us to learn from past mistakes. Not only the ones have we made on a regular basis but the ones our forefathers made and their ancestors as well. I stand firm by the idea that the times change, people don't change.

Lying there trying to convince myself to get out of bed I think to myself what is the point? Why do we constantly cram ourselves with education that no one wants to know? I thought about working everyday and the rat race we all find ourselves in. My first college year and I am already thinking to myself, what the hell is the point? If I could just take a chance to make it out on my own maybe I'd get out of this funk I'm in.

What does a man have in life? What does a man own? The ideas of having to wake up everyday and go to a job you hate sucks. Then you get home and have to hand your money over to bills and things you just fucking hate. There's a big decline these days in that type of living because my generation doesn't do things that they think feel good. We are a bunch of self-centered lazy pathetic bastards who believe the world should be handed to us and love should rule. In fact, I fall into that category too. Maybe I am exaggerating things a bit, but I am almost never wrong about anything. How often do we sit and wonder the meaning of life and in the end just finds us in complete confusion? There's no point in doing any of this. We all live and we all die, that's the only thing we all have in common. Right?

Sometimes I believe whole-heartedly we live in a world where people are just walking viruses waiting to die. Other days, I think people are a beautiful creation of God and we are meant to enjoy one another. These thoughts usually depend on the type of day I'm having. For example, if my car won't start up in the morning for no apparent reason then when I get into town I hit every traffic light around and when I get home I check the mail and realize I owe a doctor or some type of person money I am likely to hate everything around me and be a total ass to everyone. But, if I wake up and I get a refund check from the school and there isn't some sort of catastrophe happening in the family I am likely to believe the best in the world.

It's quite ironic that I sit here and lecture my own mind on how to live its own lives when the woman (once again using that term loosely) that I had wakened up to wasn't quite eighteen. Just a few years off the mark, yet still illegal. She was someone who was more lost in the world everyone else lived in and not her own. That's what struck me so much about this girl.

The whole ironic part of my experience with her was just that, it was an experience. Though, several years younger than me, this girl had been with more men than most females are with in a lifetime. For obvious reason for being nervous, I never thought that I'd have a tough time sexually pleasing a sixteen-year-old girl. It was easy to attract someone who is younger than you and it also makes it much easier when that person is a broken teen who loves nothing more than the sensation of a dick in her. She had been with guys much older than me and she had rarely been with guys her own age. So it was hard for me to view the competition. She viewed the situation like many before hand. A one-night stand? Or a long lasting relationship? Either way she wanted it, it didn't matter to me because that night would only be one time, unless I went on another long drought then I just might reconsider.

My initial meeting with this soon to be woman was at a friend's college where high school girls took it upon themselves to show up uninvited, as this was a common part of their party scene. It's also a common part to have raunchy sex with them. I knew I had an instant attraction to her just by the way she was sitting on the couch while pretending she likes her alcoholic drink. If she wanted to achieve the great feeling of being shit faced drunk she should have took the usual college way and slammed a few shots straight, but I think that would have led to her eventual vomiting. It didn't take a student with a GPA above 3.0, which I didn't have, to figure my night with her was going to be eventful because the moment I slid my fingers into her vagina she was already half way there. Once again I wondered just how much I could possibly get away with.

One of the many things that stuck in my mind about her was the scar that was located just above her clit and how it strangely enough looked sexy and yet painful at the same time. The cadaverous lady made sure that I knew she wasn't new at this. It was as though, that was her only goal in this whole ordeal. As sad as it was to say I spent half of my ten minutes of fucking wanting to know how the hell it got there. I don't think it was proper bedroom conversation or dinner conversation for that matter.

I could sit and pick her apart for hours, but the truth

is even though I was right about her, in the end I felt a great remorse. She was a girl born and raised on the outskirts of the city. Her parents who split up when she was at the age of thirteen never took the time to get to know their own flesh and blood. You would think one would get tired of the same old stereotypes after awhile but we never get tired of anything. Nostalgia is our most beloved pastime.

Patricia loved anything that involved trouble and despair. She loved ruining married men's lives and breaking the hearts of teenage boys. A young woman finds out very early on in life that she can get anything she wants in the simplest purest god given ways. Not through hard work, not through trial and error, and not through setting her mind to something. Actually all of those things are the same. She could get anything she wanted by simply spreading her legs open. Any god created man that doesn't prefer the company of other men will do anything for what's between those legs. And the girl from the broken home of hell knew that as soon as her body started to develop.

Loving the ways she was being looked at and the attention she started to get, she quickly decided to turn this into a profit. And by profit, I am not referring to money. Not yet anyway.

She could always get to the front of the line at lunch-time and she could always decide who would take her to school dances. It was like she found a magic lamp and was getting her three free wishes. All of those awkward years growing up where she was ignored by boys and neglected at home had suddenly come to a stop. At least, in school it did. Patricia might have even been a preppy bitch, but her parents never had a dime to their name so that title for her was out of the question. She wasn't fat or ugly so being gothic never really came into play either. She wasn't very book smart and was never innocent so being the quiet smart girl that most guys in junior high think about while jerking off wasn't an option either.

But, what she could be was something none of those other girls were. And that was the answer to any high school guys dream. She was essentially the whore. Once again, a girl figures out at some point in there life that to get anything they want they just have to make themselves available to the public. Tricia fucked better and longer than any girl and she fucked better than most of the female teachers. Her fucking skills were in a league of her own. So, that's who she became.

Not because she wanted to be that, but because she had to be that. Everyone thinks that it's so easy for a young person to follow the rules and do what's right. You and I know that that's bullshit. She was very popular but only by the guys that is. The girls hated her. The girls really hated her. The few so called friends she had that were girls did nothing but stab her behind the back every time she wasn't around to defend herself. Then again she wouldn't have defended herself. Physically she couldn't defend herself so when a girl made a rude remark about her she would just hope that it would go away and not turn into her being beaten up. The attitude she portrayed was priceless. It was definitely an Oscar performance. The part that killed her inside was that her parents never even had a clue that their daughter was slowly on her way to getting every type of herpes and aids a girl can attract. They were always too busy and concerned with their own lives that thinking of the human being they brought into this world never crossed their minds. Sadly enough, Patricia knew this all too well.

What started eating me away recently was the rush of kids to grow up. And the fucking laws that stand around men. Not women because when a woman does something perverted its sexy and she's just fulfilling a fantasy of the teenage boy. Girls once again know how to use their body and at a young age they doll themselves up to look much older and desirable instead of dressing like a girl that you know is taboo to touch. If a human is developed shouldn't they have the choice to have sex with whoever wants to have sex with them? God created us to have sex with the opposite sex. So why then should we be punished by it? Because the law decides everything is fine and dandy at the age of eighteen? How many men and women's lives have been ruined because of this? Yes even women.

If the thoughts I am thinking is sin and wrong than I only have God to blame. I am indeed a creation of him. That's right; I am a creation of GOD. But, my argument ends here because our thoughts aren't his. Though, all of our thoughts aren't our own. So I guess I win.

Though Patricia looked older than sixteen, I knew she wasn't over that ripe age of eighteen. Though a little more than a year and four months away from it she was still sixteen. She was also the type of girl that loved to be with an older man. Seducing her was the easiest thing that I have ever done and I had no pride in doing it whatsoever. She had this part in her that I saw and I'm sure that I was the only one who saw it.

There was this innocent side of her that no amount of screwing and dope could take away. This side of her was as deep as the ocean of thoughts I drown in on a day-to-day basis. Patricia suffered a lifelong absence of love and it was the only thing that she ever craved. Her early teenage years of sex and drug abuse were just the iceberg of what was to follow.

She sat on the edge of the bed and just starred out of the window and in her eyes I could see tears being held back and an undying willingness to have what everyone around her seemed to have. Its funny how easy things are? I don't mean easy in a sinful way but easy as in everyone wants the same things out of life. Our thoughts are so juvenile at times and at the end of the day we still desire the same things.

You can take many different people from many different backgrounds in life and below the surface you will find that their feelings aren't as foreign as the places they were born. We are not merely people living in a world; we are individuals just trying to do the best with what we have in life. People just want to be loved. And Patricia was no different.

That night was the only night I would spend with her or so I thought and hoped. I spent the next few weeks dodging text messages, e-mails, and phone calls. Sometimes she would even just stop by my place to which I would find several reasons in my head why I couldn't open the door.

She was wrapped up in a world that I didn't want to live in. She needed someone and someone to provide comfort and I wasn't that person. The truth was I was just another person that she fucked and would never see again. If I had realized the self-esteem and personal loss I had caused her I would probably still have done that. Why? Because I was lost in my own state of confusion and never would have given it a deep thought, at least that's what I have been told. She also had other baggage I didn't want and that was she did lines of cocaine like a seasoned 1970's rock star.

Anyways, after leaving the place it was a nice Sunday afternoon in college town. I drove through the streets and on the radio was none other than the song California Dreamin and it seemed so fitting. Cruising slowly down the streets I paid much attention to the people walking along the sidewalks. In particular, I was looking at the girls that were scattered everywhere around. I noticed all the differences in the people and girls. The high schools girls in whom I was interested in because of the simple fact that I had stated above were all dressed to kill. And they knew it. The college girls were a little bit more conserved, dressing in mostly sweatpants along with their hair pulled back in a ponytail. They were a dime a dozen. Nothing about any of these girls said unique, with the girls in high school most the time the message being sent was pathetic. Who was I to talk or complain though, when I enjoyed it?

The constant thoughts that ran through my mind on a day to day basis led me to wondering why girls and guys also, but not guys so much because any guy will take any girl for the most part; but why do girls when they are young constantly want to chase after an older guy and somehow believe that it makes them more mature? But latter on in life they want their lover to be younger. Why are humans so damn complicated?

In my mind I knew that I hadn't gotten any better looking from when I was young in high school but somehow it was easier to do the things I am doing now than it was back then, just for the simple fact that I am older shouldn't have made the difference.

This all led me back to my childhood while I was out at recess and trying to find myself on the better side of Hannah, she was the girl every guy in that class had wanted and she knew she could pick and choose whoever were her friend and boyfriend. Even though those boyfriends usually lasted anywhere from five to ten days the forever relationships took about just two weeks to complete.

Hannah cleverly shot me down as I leaned in for a kiss. I guess the lunch I devoured left an unpleasant odor to my breath. I still found my attempt to be successful because it was the closest I got physically to a girl. Unfortunately for Hannah, she was one of those girls who somehow hit her peak very early on it was all downhill from there. At least she witnessed a few nice years of beauty, though for our generation that all could be fixed with a few expensive surgeries.

The drive was a nice one because I finally had time to clear my mind and try to pull myself together and get back on track. After all, I had a few tests coming up and I always hated walking into the dorms late and having the damn student R.A.'s staring at me like I just got caught with my pants down.

Upon arriving, I thought about Patricia a little more than I should have. The thoughts ranged anywhere from being terrified of getting arrested to wanting to do it again.

I believe Alice Cooper said it right when he sang ever so softly "Only Women Bleed". Remember though, women know how to use their body to get what they want. It doesn't matter who they are on the inside or the experiences they have lived, all women know how to use their body. And, Patricia was just getting started.

<u>Runaway Train</u>

When I look through your eyes
I see a side no ones ever seen
Swimming is every tear
Dropping from your eyes
Every broken heart cries
Days are like numbers
And hours are your lies

Waiting on the phone
Walking in the rain all alone
Bleeding every feeling ever shown
While I'm lying in this bed
Sitting here on my own
Locked up in this home

I see you out on the streets
What do you think it does to me?
To know your hearts never missed a beat
Shaking hands with fake smiles
Knowing hes taken your love a mile

Don't know what to say
Never knew what to do
All I know is I wanted to get close to you
On this runaway train tonight

Chapter 3
Snow Blind

Arriving to class fifteen minutes late the professor managed to mark me down as being absent even though I stayed the rest of the boring life draining class. He was the only professor that I had that semester that treated every living thing like it was garbage and he was above us all. This guy was bald headed and had this goatee that he had spent every week applying just for men to. The fact that he had no hair on his head and gray back hair made him take his frustration out on the youth that didn't want to be in that class.

We had to hand in our one page paper on what we thought was the most corrupt thing in the world today, just something this guy could read after class that allowed him to pry into our thoughts just a little bit more than he already had. Sometimes I thought to myself, this guy probably only became a professor to stay close to the youth while he wallowed away in his own emptiness in life. My paper consisted of Satan and God, the most controversial subject to ever found its way on this planet. For once that bald headed prick gave me my best grade yet in the class and that was my hard earned B+.

"They Satan has blended into many forms in which he takes place in. He walks amongst civilians every second of every day. Some believe that there are demons in all the parts of the world. I believe in this notion quite wholeheartedly. You see, I know many of these demons by their first names and have spent many nights waking up next to them or dreaming about them.

The notions and beliefs in Satan have always fascinated me with no end. We are taught to be aware of such a spirit, person, some form or figure. We know he is the living hell and is full of lies and deceitfulness. I have always had what The Rolling Stones sang sympathy for the devil. I think we know very little about this creature and we all just choose to hate and resent him. But in fact, we indulge ourselves in Satan every single chance we get. We love sin beyond any type of measure. Maybe we are the living-breathing devil in this world. We each hold a part of him in us that we just can't let go because if we do we feel like we lose our adventure and excitement in life. Satan and sin brings a lot of attention to us and our inner ambitions and desires. Satan and we have a very strong reliable love affair that has been going on for ages. Actually, since the beginning of time we have had this love affair with the beast.

Everyday I look in the mirror I see a beast that won't go away. Some call it as having a monkey on your back but I see it as a beast. And there are times though I look in the mirror and I see a perfect creation of God. That's only because I have to sleep at night.

We here God's side of the story all the time, yet we never hear Satan's side of the story. We are always to assume God knows what's best for us. When you look around though at the world you see a civilization about to go up in smoke. Satan ever since his fall from grace has tried to get back into heaven and rule. Just maybe though he is content in hell and after all of this time he has learned to cope with it. Just like we learn to cope with the cards we are dealt with in life. If we are in a tragic accident and are permanently damaged in it we learn to cope with it. If we lose a loved one, we are told to cope with it. If you have had to spend of minute of your life in a living hell you are told to cope with it. Well I'm tired of coping with life and all of its bullshit. I need a change. But there's just one more thought that keeps haunting me inside

29

and that's what if Satan is the one in charge these days and God has fallen."

As I stumbled my way out of the classroom I thought how nice it would be to get away from this freezing cold hellhole for a while. Maybe even move out to California or some place where your dick didn't become half of its god given size every time you step foot outside. The wind was blowing hard in my face and as I headed back to the dorm I laughed inside at everyone rushing to get in their classrooms without having their hair torn apart.

I wondered how any girl could manage to wear a skirt like this on a day that was bitterly miserable to be outside. I also took notice how almost every guy on campus tried going for some type of look that they thought brought coolness. I thought for sure the Kurt Cobain look was out and there was also the never dying hippie style that people thought they needed to be because they were tired of society and their rules.

What most of these people didn't realize was that they never witnessed a real problem in their lives. Just because your father comes home drunk and will talk for hours doesn't mean you have it bad or just because everyone you know takes medication to help them sleep or shit, doesn't make them an addict to be aware of. Still these hippie/Bob Marley wannabes were the most fun to talk to on campus. Their constant speeches of how corrupt everything was kept me interested only while I was stoned. Which didn't happen as often as I would have liked, these people's stories ranged from being brought up to be racist to their dad not paying enough attention to them while playing pee wee football. They preached without end about how they would never make these same mistakes.

Sitting back at my room I consistently dreamt of getting away and starting over. I didn't care about whether or not I finished school or not, it wasn't a priority for me anymore.

The thought of leaving everything behind and starting over began to have a strong appeal to me. One that I hoped one day would follow through. Sitting around in the same old town all the time is just one of the most depressing things I have been doing to myself. It's a suicide plain and simple. It reminds me a lot of that line in Tom Petty's Here Comes My Girl song. You know, the line that goes

You know, sometimes, I don't know why,
But this old town just seems so hopeless
I aint really sure, but it seems I remember the good times
Were just a little bit more in focus

As I walked into my college doom room I saw the ever-mysterious James. I often wondered how James got by doing the things that he was so ever famous for. How did someone function to a high degree on such little sleep? He never slept. At nights he was gone living the college life and by morning he was in class and by the afternoon he was back drinking himself away to heaven. Still he functioned better and quicker than anyone I ever knew. His G.P.A was hovering around a three point four and his lack of sleep never got in the way.

James was the man that every guy tried to be on campus. He simply had it all. From getting college girls wet, to the life of the party, he was someone everyone envisioned himself or herself being. One night in particular James and I decided to hit the town and stop by a few parties. Well, the first few weeks of the school year most college parties are open to anyone that wants to come in. The fraternities wanted people to show because they needed individuals for their sad, hard to get laid, tree house club. These parties are swarming with young females looking to make some new friends. It's the perfect opportunity for a guy who simply just wants to get laid. These freshmen girls are away from home for the first time and they are now thrown into an environment that is basically foreign to them.

Unlike at home where they are safe and don't have the urge to venture far from what they know, college is a place to experiment with everything. Most girls when they first get to college have only received limited sexual experiences. Unless you were Patricia and her clan of dick humping bandits who were on their way to making big bucks doing it. Most of the females have been fingered and had the occasional ten second sex from their lack luster boyfriend. When college arrives something inside of them changes, and it changes in everyone who gets on that campus for the first time. Girls start having sex with girls and guys started fulfilling nasty fetishes that they have for so long wanted to explore. Well upon arriving at this particular party, James had plenty of friends at this school and like I mentioned before everyone loved him.

The party scenery was anything but inspiring, it was a basement that was hotter than hell and it was jam packed with people and the only thing anyone there had in common was what they were drinking out of their nice little red cups. My observation and best judgment told me to wait another hour or so to make any moves for best results.

Not feeling too comfortable when I got there I decided the best way to loosen up would mean downing a few drinks and letting Mother Nature kick in. Meanwhile, James was already getting down to business. He was out of sight within those first ten minutes meaning he was occupying a room and also occupying a lady who had so eagerly attended the party.

So standing there trying to look cool with that attitude that went along with my clothing that stated, "I don't care, but I do enough to get what I want". I tried to look as smooth as a skinny sweaty white guy could. Like I mentioned before, college parties are more opened during those first few weeks because they are trying to draw people in and want you to join their ever so homosexual group. Finally, getting the courage to walk up to someone, that someone meaning a girl who I thought would be easy to score with and closer to my own age than Patricia I asked how she was enjoying the party. She looked up at me and asked are you pledging? Like I naïve jackass I am at times I asked what do you mean? She then replied are you joining this frat? Now before I go any further I think I should mention that at times like these it is best to lie to get what you really want. I should've taken my uncles advice when he said, sometimes in life you need to tell half-truths. Well looking back at her drunken state hoping she was just drunk enough to let me do the things to her body that I so desperately wanted to do she gave me a dirty look, chuckles to herself and just left.

This pissed me off more so than I could possibly explain. Here I was at a party I had no business being at and everyone is in their clicks and here I am with my thumb up my ass looking like I'm busy and have it together. Also, my roommate is upstairs giving some girl the ride of her life. So, like any mentally stable person I decided that I was going to pledge. But, pledging was something I was going to do under my own terms. You see I didn't want to be in this frat so I was going to do things a little different. Like I said, I pledged. I pledged six beers worth of piss all over the sofa and on the door handles of every cocksuckers bedroom. It made me feel quite good, not because I did something gross that I felt needed to be done, I felt good because I just unloaded a bladder full of urine. It feels nice when you get that out of your system.

That would be the end of my night or so I thought. Coming out of that basement which could have easily passed for a torture chamber I ran into two girls who I was somewhat familiar with at school. The girls were Mia and Dani. Mia was a girl who I had seen briefly each week walking out of the same building that I had my math class in and Dani was a girl in my Spanish class and possible two others who always seemed to get to class fifteen minutes before the teacher and she had to make sure she always finished her tests first and along with that her hand was always the first one to go up in the air whenever there was a question to be asked.

Mia was the wilder one between the two and most the time she made the plans for Dani on the weekends. Even though, Dani was a much smarter girl she never possessed the self-confidence and assertiveness that ones needs to lead their own life. Mia at times was a mere tease. She loved to flirt around and pretend to have the fun to persuade people to pay more attention to her but in reality she rarely did anything sexual and spent most nights to her despite what everyone else thought. She was a taller girl that had a very distinctive pretty face. High cheekbones, large hazel eyes, long skinny legs, and her chest were just the right size. She possessed long black hair and her lips were never a strong point for her considering they were always chapped. Still, I always found her to be a fun person to spend any type of time with and apparently she felt the same about me.

Dani was a pretty girl who had her own attractive traits but often times found her overshadowed by Mia. She spent many weekends at parties just trying to find her place in the whole scheme of things. Dani was the girl that guys usually went after once they failed at their first choice. This wasn't because she wasn't pretty but she never possessed that certain quality or trait that someone finds intriguing and for that she never was anyone's first choice. While she could be talkative she usually wasn't. Dani would only open up and talk if she knew you very well and that wasn't often. She never took the time to get to know anyone on campus very well and she was quite content with the few friends she had. I don't know if she viewed that part of herself as a positive or negative quality.

Dani had long brown hair and green eyes. Her face was usually on the pale side and she rarely showed her legs. She did have this walk that was unique. Her right leg would bend slightly in and it was in a strange way sexy. Her height was of average and she wasn't too keen on ever wearing anything that showed too much skin or cleavage. Something that I found very respectable since most girls these days dress like they are ready to give you a price for an hour spent in the back of your vehicle. That was another thing that I found very interesting. Many people took her for someone who was stuck up but this couldn't be further from the truth. She was just shy and didn't exactly know how to mingle with people she had just met. This was college and the life she knew and loved so much in high school was over. Even though, she would say every chance she got that she was happier than hell that high school was over she never really meant that. Dani was just another girl who felt lost after she graduated, she was another girl who had it all during her four glorious years in high school and now was finding it hard to make that transaction into college. Her momentum of popularity never carried over. And to make matters worse she was always playing second fiddle to Mia or any other girl she was with for the night.

So on my way out of the party they decided it would be fun to walk with me back to campus. The air was unusually cold for this time of year, but the alcohol consumption made it a lot more possible to walk back. My drinks had made my body invincible to the outdoor conditions.

Walking back with me was something I wasn't opposing to. They were in the best state they could be and that was drunk. Being the gentleman I was my first intention was to take advantage of the situation but something inside of me changed and I decided for future meetings with them it would be best to keep it in my pants and that's just exactly what I did unfortunately. They had the usual drunk girl attitude and tone of voice. Both Mia and Dani were now loud, reckless, and saying things they would latter regret. I guided them from now falling off the sidewalk and into the street where they would have been hit and most likely killed, making the attraction then impossible for me.

The best thing about being drunk and the surrounding yourself with drunken people when you are indeed under the influence is that you know what you are doing is wrong but you don't care. Most everyone says I didn't mean that and that's not how I feel. That my friend is complete bullshit and luckily for you I'll tell you why. People don't all of sudden lose everything that's true to themselves when they are drunk and become this person that never existed inside of them before. Alcohol just allows you to bring out that person in you that you try so desperately to hide on a day-to-day basis.

Alcohol is like an escape from your reality and a trip into what you just want to express but can't ever seem to work up the courage to convey. People fuck when they're drunk because the human body is made to have sex and people desire sex all the time. I'm not different from the population on that and people think about it more often then you think. Most people think that they are the only ones with certain desires and wants in life, that couldn't be further from the truth. Another point on alcohol is that it is by far the best icebreaker. How many memories do you have with people past the age of eighteen that you never met before that didn't in someway start at a party and someone being opened to talk because they are drunk? Its ashame the amount of bad rap that alcohol gets these days. It's not the drink that's hurting you it's the constant denial in oneself and empty space that you ever so want to fulfill. Also, some people are most enjoyable when they are drunk and that's something also comforting to know.

Dani was especially feeling the effects of alcohol. I knew this was something she rarely did and it showed by the way she was acting. Spilling her guts out about how much pressure she is under from her parents to do well. And how her mother just never lets up about her not becoming a failure in life. It was well planted in her mind that if she didn't graduate college and also at the top of her class than she basically failed at life. Dani went on for the longest time walking back to campus about how much she hated the pressure and didn't feel like she could do it anymore. In my mind, I felt remorse for her but I also said to myself for her own benefit that tomorrow when all of this is said and done that I would act like noting happened and that she didn't reveal her inner most feelings. Because it's not right for someone to be drunk and tell you their feelings without you being drunk and spilling your guts out too.

Meanwhile, Mia was laughing hysterically the whole time and this was something that got old pretty quick. I always thought myself capable of making others laugh but not to the point where some girl needed to repeat every five seconds that I'm funny and to tell that one joke again. Something I apparently said three weeks ago in class. It was a little flattering to know she remembered something so pointless about me.

Mia was a little bit more seasoned when it came to drinking then Dani. In fact, she was getting tired of Dani's constant rampant talk. Expressing what most likely were her true feelings Mia so gently yelled just shut the fuck up; nobody cares about your pristine life and your damn pressure from your lesbian mother. Feeling quite embarrassed for Dani I just pretended I didn't hear anything. This wasn't the best option because I would have to be deaf not to hear Mia's latest bitch.

I guess from hearing Mia talk that Dani's mom was a man trapped in a woman's body and wanted too bad to be with another woman and leave her father. This was something that I had no business knowing and it did change how I viewed Dani now. To me from then on I felt bad for her and just didn't know what to say to her. Dani was a girl that was never meant to be born. Her parents never really wanted her and the birth was an apparent mistake. I don't think that her mom regretted having Dani in her life I think she just regretted the lie that she decided to live on a day-to-day basis. This once again was none of my business. Her mother back in the day was just a confused girl who found herself more attracted to women than men and unfortunately the first and only time she would experiment with having sex with a man it led to her pregnancy. In addition to that, in those times it wasn't acceptable for someone not to be heterosexual. So to cover up her own insecurities and embarrassment she decided to marry Dani's eventual father.

Her father was someone who just wanted to get laid and get laid is exactly what he did. It would in his own mind be the biggest mistake of his life. He was indeed attracted to Dani's mother but never loved her and he lived in a time where if you got someone pregnant that meant you definitely had to get married and ultimately deal with what you did. It's strange that her parents only had sex that one time and to deal with their terrible decision they got drunk quite often and Dani's father for sure wasn't going to spend the rest of his life not getting any pussy. He would do what so many great men out there do and that was cheating on his wife. He made it a ritual to fuck as many hopeless women he could. This however would never hurt her mother because she wanted to be out in about eating pussy like it was going out of style, but she didn't do it that often. She spent the majority of her time raising Dani and putting the most ridiculous pressure on her to perform great in whatever she attempted or didn't attempt to do.

She spent her whole life living up to expectations

that got higher through each minor accomplishment. That's the trouble with parents and their undying desire to make their children into people they never were. The ironic thing, which I love, is when people have children that turn out to be the very kid in school they picked on. How do parents then deal with the disappointments that they created and brought into this world?

We spend our whole entire life looking in from the outside that we don't realize is that we are stuck on the inside. And while we are doing this we spend countless years criticizing other people and doing everything we can to downtrodden other people. I think the reason we waste so much time on other people and their so called faults is that we are so disgusted and embarrassed of ourselves that it might just be way too painful to deal with. Why take the time out and find why you are such a fucking freak for doing the shit you do instead of driving another nail into the people in this world that God himself has damned.

God, now that's a word that gets misused a lot. How can an all knowing and loving creator be so ignorant and heartless at times. Look at all the trouble and heartache in this world. There are countries that are in fact a living hell. There ways of life are so fucking shitty and sad that when I see it I literary break down in tears. How can God just turn his back on people? Not only did God turn his back on people but also he does it to innocent little children. It's nobody's fault that they get born into a world that does nothing but shit on them. Children don't ask to be born into a world where there parents don't give a damn about them or their parents are just embarrassed by the way their kids turned out. And how about all these people that just claim that all you have to do is trust God and his love will prevail. These people need to wake the fuck up because they are living in a fantasy world. These are usually the same people that are fucking some child whose years from going through puberty. We put this trust into leaders and people that claim to be men of God, yet they are the ones that are corrupting the world beyond means.

Granted, I have explored the Internet in a lot of sinful ways. But, unlike these freaks of nature I don't hurt anyone or break the law. Well, there was the sixteen-year-old girl, or woman, or girl. It's all too much of a blur honestly.

Finally, we arrived to their dorm and both Mia and Dani found it necessary to French kiss me. I was happy and thought the night to be successful even with that tease of a good time. I continued my way to my dorm and feeling a little exhausted I decided just to site outside of the building before I entered it. Sitting there I was greeted by the Bob Dylan wannabes of the school and their Yoko Ono wannabe girls. The one girl there that probably spent years convincing herself that this was her click and kind of people invited me into their room to have a few drinks and just hang out. I didn't have anything else better to do so I graciously accepted the invitation to the room. Sitting on the bed were some misfits and the girls there weren't much to jerk off to. I will say that everyone was over friendly and made me feel like my presence meant something when all of us knew that it didn't mean a damn thing.

The girl that supposedly had fooled around with the majority of the guys and girls there wanted to make her available to me. Feeling a little hopeless from the night due to the embarrassment at the party and the baby sitting I did on my walk back I felt this would be just the right thing to turn my night around. Sitting next to me on the bed she openly put her hand on my thigh and continued to move it up and down my leg and eventually caressing my dick. I was getting harder than a twelve year old watching his first porno, so we both decided that this would be something that had to be taken care of.

Sprinting up the steps to get to my room, which were

quite a few floors above theirs we just decided to make our appointment in the elevator. Hoping like hell not to lose myself before the actual business started I did what I could to kill the attraction for a moment. Imagining her to be some disgusting woman, but that wouldn't work. Thinking I was going to get laid turned out to be the wrong thought and this girl decided it would be most appropriate to suck on my cock. She did so with great momentum and style. It didn't take long to burst and after that she still wasn't satisfied and wanted to continue in my room.

Upon arriving to my room, James had already had the place occupied with his lady of the night. I didn't even have to knock on anything I could hear the girl screaming all the way down the hall. So I jumped to my next option and that was a key that James gave to me before the night started. James had recently moved out of his previous room to stay with me and still had the extra key that he never turned in. And the guy who had the room was always gone for the weekends and with that I had the magical idea to occupy his room.

With one of the beds opened I took the empty bed and continued to do what I had hoped I was going to do the entire night. This time it was different because I never had been with a gothic/Yoko Ono wannabe/1960's hippie wannabe. The girl could fuck better than anyone I ever had encountered. She insisted on being on top and all the while her boobs were bouncing viciously up and down and the sweat was pouring off of her. I wrapped my arm around her waist and forced the fucking much harder than it already was. Her hair was flipping back and forth and as soon as she came she jumped off of me, quickly put her pants back on, smiled, and left. The strangest experience yet. And at least this time it was with someone over that ripe age of eighteen.

For the next week or so this mysterious girl would show up and we spend time getting high and fucking. Those were the only two things we had in common and I didn't mind at all. Also, she always had this funky moan to her every time I managed to have any contact with her vagina, kind of like she was giving birth to a fifteen-pound baby. Either it was a good sign on my part or she just really needed to get off.

Following our casual meetings together she would show me the proper way of snorting coke. This was something I was foreign to and didn't partake much in, becoming a drug addict was just something I wasn't too keen of doing.

However, the few times we would do it she would insist on lying on her back and having me snort the blow off of her stomach. I hated doing that, it was never pleasant and I constantly ended up with a bloody nose and a high I wanted to come off of real quickly. The last time she left I just sat on the floor and eventually dragged myself onto my bed where I always did my best thinking. Something about being high made my brainwork on a level I wasn't accustomed to.

Lying in bed that night I just thought about everything. I started to wonder how my life had gotten to the point to where it was. When did everything become so out of line in my life? Closing my eyes it was so easy to find myself being a child again. I just wish the good times would outweigh the bad ones. It seems as though people as a society let the bad times outweigh everything in their life. It's funny how no matter how many positive compliments a person gets in life it's only the hurtful ones we remember with clarity. That's because all the good things in life we let run together as one well-lived period instead of capturing those feelings and keeping them.

Life isn't meant to be hurtful and lived in complete disarray. It's in ourselves that we find that we are meant to be forgiven, but everyone else shouldn't have that same opportunity. That and when someone does something harsh to someone else we think that the person should be forgiven and that others hold onto their pain too long. People just can't seem to get and understand that we are all the same. We all like to think we are all unique and that no one truly understands the real beauty in us but that's bullshit. We all feel what others hide. Another thought crossed my mind that night and it was love.

What is love? And why do so many people put a positive look on it all the time? People seem to always paint a heart full of passionate red. When in most cases it should be painted in all pure black. Love isn't such a beautiful thing when you know it to its fullest extent. In many ways, it is like a disease that sleeps in your soul and slowly eats away at you until you are insane. The pain of love is something that far outweighs the pain of anything else you will ever witness or feel.

Love can either be an awakening or a reality block. It doesn't always bring out the best in you and in a lot of cases it will bring out the monster in you. It will make you do things you never dreamed of. People live and die for love, unfortunately when they die for love they often find themselves just going through the motions in life. Sort of like they are on autopilot. The pain of the constant reminder of what you don't have or in some cases never will have plays out like a sick twisted game in your mind. And all the while you start to miss out on what is enjoyable in life. The thought that without that missing piece in your life you will never be satisfied. That my friend is complete bullshit. Society has shown us that it's not okay to feel pain.

Pain is just another emotion just like everything else and it comes in cycles. We will all witness this. We spend countless dollars every year on items to make us happy and on prescription medicine. You don't need it, I tell myself all the time. You just don't need it. Embrace your pain like it's your best friend or your all time best fuck. Pain will make you wake up twice as fast as any love out there. In the moment of pain you finally figure out just who you are on the inside. The outside of you is very easy to fake. But we spend a lifetime trying to figure out who we are on the inside, because we only feel what is on the inside and not what represents us on the outside. We are taught that the outside is what really matters. There is plenty of help out there that focuses on losing weight, having bigger tits, and yes now we even have to have giant cocks. The pills out there that will make your penis larger and more productive. As to say, what God gave you isn't pleasing to no one and if you want to be in a league of your own then this pill will do that for you. And women, have it a million times worse than men. Women constantly have to be beautiful all the time and anything less just shows that they don't care about anything.

The television shows show this all the time. Especially programs for years ago like Leave it to Beaver, The Brady Bunch, and even on Gilligan's Island the women are dress to make you want to fuck them in the worse way possible. Well for me the two ladies and not Mrs. Howell. Yes, women know this and they spend their whole lives trying to find the fountain of youth. Men just want their cocks to be bigger.

Back to my notion on love, it's not always bleak, as I have described it. It can be the best thing to have ever happen to you. Whether it works out for the better or not, everyone should witness it at least once. Actually, God wants you to witness it just one time. But, why take advice from something that can't even run their own planet, right?

Still lying in bed I started to dream again. . As I was lying in my bed, I drifted off to sleep. And in my dream I went back in time. I saw and talked to everyone who had an impact on my life and I was in the body of a child because that was the time period I had fallen into. In my dream, I knew I was back in time. My mind was present day, yet my body wasn't. The visions of conversation with deceased loved ones were touching and surroundings were so surreal.

I couldn't believe it; I thought I had accomplished what man has dreamt of doing since the beginning of time. I saw my grandparent's house and my family and their friends also. I was at my old elementary school playing touch football with my father and childhood friend. And in between plays I was talking to a girl who in reality I never knew too much about and her impact in my life wasn't significant or so I thought. The skies were unusually gray as if there was a portal to get me back to my time.

As I woke up, I thought about that dream the whole entire day. It's strange how something that isn't real can have such an everlasting effect on you. Dreams are like a reality and fantasy that we want so much yet never seem to capture. Sometimes for some of us that fantasy comes true and along with dreams there are nightmares and for a lot of us that is what comes true. Do we even realize it?

The only thing that haunts me day in and day out is the woman I love. The worst part is she doesn't love me. She never did love me. We were just two different people from different places, yet we were so closely bonded through similarities. Our time was so brief that within a few months it won't surprise me if she just completely forgets about me in everyway possible. It's strange how what something means to someone can mean nothing to another. Time spent with an individual is something that can change your life forever. Whether the time spent is for a few weeks, a few months, a year, or a few years. But the moment in life when that person leaves you it feels like your heart just sunk in your chest and you can't seem to get it to stay where it should be. Maybe for a couple days you get it put back into place but the more you think about the person the more it seems to go right back where you are.

What seemed like yesterday now have been a few years. The one night spent with the person you hoped to spend the rest of your life with seemed like it went by in a blink of an eye. When that ten a.m. alarm went off I would have done anything to turn back to the night. But, the hardest part is getting past the fantasy and the realization that sometimes in life what you think is true and here to stay is all made up in your mind to make you feel better about the situation. She had a very distinct smell to her, a smell that I wanted to capture in a moment and stay in. Those feelings don't always count for something. The smell was like lilacs and some rare perfume put together. But those thoughts had to be put to rest. To move on sometimes means to do the unthinkable and that is forget. She wasn't perfect looking either, she had many flaws and I was obsessed with each and every one. Her smarts were limited and her capacity of love was always filled with lies and pain. I would have given up everything I ever knew and loved to be with her. To change her course of hurt and despair. Sometimes in life you think you found the person you want to spend the rest of your life with and then something comes along and takes it away from you and you can't begin to fathom how you ever could live without it. The love of my life lost left me searching twice as hard for something that I always thought in the back of my mind never existed. Like I said she had many flaws but I loved every single one of them. I still remember the last time I ever saw her.

There she was standing in front of me looking rather thin and worn. Her face hadn't kept the same glow to it from when I first met her. It had minor scars and scratched away pimples. Her weight decreased drastically and not in a positive way at all. Her hair was more like wire than strands of silk. Along with that, her teeth looked a little crooked also and it affected her smile to a degree. She seemed nervous to the point where she almost acted like nothing had happened between us. I didn't know how to respond so the first thing I did was kiss her right on the lips and tell her I was happy to see her. I never even asked why she came out all of this way to see me or what was going on in her life that had changed her appearance. All I knew was the girl that I had for months spent time trying to ignore and forget was back in my life. There were things I just couldn't hide from my conscience anymore and that was I was in love with her.

I often wondered how deep her feelings were for me. Was I someone she ever thought about or was I just a guy she thought wanted sex from her? I felt so foolish every time I thought about her because we didn't really know anything about one another other than what we both looked like naked. Many times I would just imagine we were together and that our relationship was strong and one that was built upon trust and love. I knew I was making a fairy tale romance that wouldn't last in anyone's life. This was a romance that I never wanted to get out of anyhow. Dealing with everyone and their opinions was a train I really didn't want to be hit by but it didn't take away from the agony and part of myself that I missed.

There is no worse feeling or thing in this world than being alone. Loneliness is the number one killer in sanity. There is nothing quite like it in this world. It makes you become one on one with yourself and you start to realize things about you that you never in the world thought to be true. Sometimes the real monster that we hide away in our days comes out and becomes the only side of us that we know. We try all the time so desperately to hide that ugly side that when in comes out and indeed it will come out in all of us at some point in our lives it destroys us. It takes our soul and heart and makes them become two different things that won't reason with one another.

It's like a disease that sleeps next to us and each morning we wake up we realize that the night before we fucked it and it starts to get closer and closer each morning. Loneliness starts then to become our only friend. It is the only thing we know and when it starts to slip away we panic in fear that we lost our only friend. When in fact, it never was a friend at all, but an enemy in disguise. What a harsh thing for humans to come to gripes with. It also makes us do things we never thought tangible. The loneliness then brings some of its best friends along to occupy us when it can't. They include paranoia and anger not to mention sweet bitterness.

They all are a division of loneliness that creeps up on us before we can stop to realize it. Yea it is a slow painful death of the soul. Once your soul is dead then your heart melts away and then your left living out or existing out the rest of your days in complete disarray. We spend countless money trying to get that living feeling back and we don't realize it until we die but no amount of money could ever bring that back so we turn to drugs and alcohol and that only makes the demon in is come alive more than ever. A life filled with depression, loneliness, and substance abuse leads to a cold death where everyone stands around at your funeral and says I never really had the chance to get to know him or her. They always seemed nice. That's no way to live or die. Life is one of the shortest rides in mankind. We don't think it is because we don't perceive ourselves past our death. In fact the moment of death can be like an awakening, a new beginning.

Sometimes in life people change. They change the way they do things. They change the way they look and the way they perceive things. But, they never change they way people, events, and things make them feel. It might lessen or strengthen but certain emotions are always there to stay. You can run from everyone and anything but you can't run from yourself or from your past.

The rest of the weekend consisted of me going back home and trying to relax and pull myself back together from the last night. Going back home I decided to spend the day with my father. Something different than most people that are at my age is that my father and I had a special relationship.

We were best friends and I knew that I could always go to him and tell him anything. He would never turn his back on me and I knew that. Sometimes I think I should have cherished him a little more than I did, but I had so much going on that it was hard to stop and realize anything that was positive in my life.

We went to play a few games of horseshoes and just catch up. It was special because it was the end of summer and with how we have seen things in life happen we knew that good things never last forever. Taking in the scenery around us we both came to the realization that there had to be a higher power. There just had to be a God somewhere that was responsible for us being there and all of the natural surroundings couldn't have just happened. Something had to be behind all of it. It was a comforting thought that led to even more realizations. And one was that I understood that my father loved me dearly. We walked around the park and talked about how similar people really are and how everyone just puts on a mask to hide their own insecurities. We finished the day by sitting on an old bridge and reminiscing on past times and times in his life when he was growing up. The differences in relationships from when he was a kid and before then and now.

People today are much closer to their children. In the past it was common and acceptable to raise a hand to a child and hurt them. Children usually didn't know much at all about their parents past and especially the time period in their parent's lives when they were rebellious. It was an unspoken thing. Families ate at the dinner table and little conversation happened. The father worked and the mother stayed at home making dinner and cleaning. Families didn't get divorces and the kids had to walk a tight rope and when they fell off of it, it usually meant getting an ass beating by the old man. Those generations decided to be different in everyway to their parents and their times by changing their clothing, music, and choice of words.

This is still true to this day. But, parents today are much more lenient on what they let their kids get away with. The youth today has no reason whatsoever to rebel and be a bunch of asshole to their elders. Today's generations need a nice swift kick in the ass and someone to set them straight. This is coming for someone that owns that generation. Born into and expected to go with it, but it is bullshit and it is pathetic in my opinion. It is not always wrong to hit a child because sometimes that is the only way they will ever learn. These pointless time outs and saying no and making threats that you never follow through with are just stepping stones for that child to break and continue to be a thorn in some teacher's ass. I could never be a teacher, especially a high school teacher because I would be too tempted by the eighteen-year-old girls that look hotter than hell. But, I couldn't be a teacher because I would be tempted to hurt a dumbass that runs their mouth thinking that there isn't going to be any consequences to follow.

Parents and their children's relationships are tight these days because parents and children share a common theme on growing up and the parents don't forget what is was like for them and how much they hated growing up under their parents rules so they see room for improvement and allow small incidents to slide by.

Everything in life is changing, the drugs, the outlets of anger, and even relationships amongst parents and children. Dani would disagree with these statements if given the chance to hear them. But I have a feeling when I return Monday morning there will be a lot of avoiding of people going on. And I'm sure Mia the so-called best friend won't let anyone forget about it.

Just a Thought

Pain is just a word full of meaning
Like a thought that leads to dreaming
No where to go when there's no one at home
That empty feeling like you're all alone

Memories that seem to always show
Some stay and others just go
No one sees because few ever know
What lies beneath a heart of stone?
Is much more than what is ever shown
Others see what you've always known

When today's tomorrow becomes yesterday
Love lies bleeding all the way
You feel what others say
Yet those thoughts just come to stay
Like the summer rain washing away
Every ache and pain of your yesterday

Chapter 4
Save Your Love

The week started off just like any other week in this town except for the fact that Dani and Mia and yes even I tried avoiding each other as much as we could. This included my usual stance when it comes to people and that is pretend that I don't see them when I am walking by or if I have to stop and engage in conversation I give the usual hello and how are you doing?

What did I have to be embarrassed about though? I'm not the one who got drunk and decided to recite my whole life story leaving out all of the positive parts or the one who decided to be loud and bitch out her current best friend. In any instance I did avoid them. I couldn't stop thinking about Dani though and if those problems she expressed or the ones Mia was so opened about explaining were actually true or not. I elected to believe they were true because people don't lie when they are drunk they are just conveying their honest unspoken feelings. Did I feel bad for her truly or did I see it as an easy way into her life and getting what I really wanted? Sex? Even so, I do think that the feelings of remorse were genuine because I just am not that kind of guy. Really, I am not that kind of guy. But, every guy has at least one thing in common.

The few times that I would see Dani since then she would take my approach and continue on walking without saying a word. I wasn't sure whether or not she didn't like me or if indeed she was embarrassed. She didn't have to be; I had so many of my own mishaps and mental anguish that it was hard for me to see exactly where everyone else's where.

Mia wasn't shy when it came to seeing me, she would give me a flirtatious wave and hello and just temp me to talk about that stupid walk that was essentially pointless. Mia was that girl that I couldn't ever stand to be around, she always had trouble in her eye and her voice had disaster written in every tone she put it in. Thankfully, I wasn't falling in that trap yet.

During the walk back to my dorm where I would usually take a two-hour nap because I was up too late the night before and unlike James I couldn't function without a certain amount of sleep. This time would be a little bit different though; as I looked down at my phone I didn't recognize the number at all. And to this day I regret it but I decided to call the number and to my surprise the person on the other end of the phone was none other than Patricia. Why of why God did I decide to respond back? Didn't I realize that fucking an underage girl meant going to jail and losing all of my hopes and dreams? It is something that no one other than a man could explain really. Finding good reliable pussy is quite hard. The good part isn't hard and finding the reliable part isn't hard but getting both of those combinations was the true task at hand. Patricia was both of those and resisting her was harder than Rosie O'Donnell not jerking off after watching the season finale of The Facts of Life.

Patricia had this hold on me that was so damn hard to break. She was the type of girl that was opened to doing anything that would please you. She looked at exploring sexually just made her that much harder to say no to and she was absolutely correct. Still jail was no place for me. I have never been to keen to the idea of actually meeting a big black guy named Bubba.

When a guy sees something he likes it takes every-thing he has not to give into temptation. That's why the Internet is such a useful item. That is, until you have someone check your history on it and that just leaves you opened to explaining. For a man to resist a girl is something once again only a man can understand, especially a piece of ass that was considered wrong by the world. Even knowing all of this I still decided to give her a call.

Speaking frantically she cried over the phone that she left home to follow her heart, which apparently led her to me. How she found out about my whereabouts is beyond me. Stunned I grab my things and flew out of the dorm and raced to meet her. Cruising through the city with the windows down and the radio blasting I was in a relatively great mood. I don't know why but something about her got to me. To explain it would take me time that I don't have. Thoughts were racing through my mind like what was she going to look like? Was I gone long enough for her to change at all? The moment came that I finally arrived.

As I pulled into the parking lot of the local mall I got out of the car that belonged to James. A 2006 red Ferrari. Because knowing I was going to see her I wanted to create the impression that I was something to desire. When in reality I didn't own a damn thing other than my name. Too much of my surprise she wasn't even fucking there. I looked around and around but she was nowhere to be found.

Knowing what I do know about her I just figured she went off with the nearest hairy penis she could find. The taboo girl couldn't even show me the common courtesy to wait and greet me after the phone call that we had. Its ashame when you build yourself up for something that doesn't blossom to what you wanted. Feeling like the dumbass that I often was I just sat on the hood of my car for an extra half hour hoping that just maybe I wasn't as big as a fool as I was. My mind went rapidly back to the one measly night that I had spent with her. A sixteen-year-old high school girl that I had seduced and decided to throw to the curb once I was done with her. But, what if I wasn't actually done with her. Maybe

I felt something that night that I had never felt before. Every time I thought of her name or face something inside of me lit up and came alive. I knew that it was something that had to be restrained because she was too young for me but damn it felt good.

The moment of when I felt her warm wet pussy on my dick was the only thing keeping me staying in hopes of seeing her. That's what I wanted to make myself believe. As the moment came that I decided to get back into the car I was so ever proud to drive I looked up and saw her calling my name as she quickly ran over. I couldn't believe it, after all the time that had elapsed I was feeling nervous. My palms began to get sweaty and the way I wanted to stand to look cool only made me fidget around. I kept clearing my throat because I didn't want any part of my speech to crack. I hate it when my voice still cracks. I was dead set against pulling a Peter Brady incident.

There she was standing in front of me with the look that got me wanting her right from the get go. Her face was absolutely caked with makeup that she apparently hadn't learn how to master applying to her face and she this smell to her that drove me crazy, kind of like the smell the girl that I spent so much time loving had. Her weight had increased a little but it wasn't something so drastic that anyone other than me would have noticed because I'm the type of person that somehow notices everything on another person. Her hair looked wild sort of like she had been running in the wind awhile. Along with that, her teeth were pearl white and perfectly straight due to the braces she use to hate wearing.

Patricia seemed nervous to the point where she almost acted like nothing had happened between us. I didn't know how to respond so the first thing I did was kiss her right on the lips and tell her I was happy to see her. I never even asked why she came out all of this way to see me or what was going on in her life that had changed her appearance. All

I knew was the girl that I had for months spent time trying to ignore and forget was back in my life. There were things I just couldn't hide from my conscience anymore and that was I possibly falling in love with her.

We drove around the city awhile and the conversation between us was more of like a conversation between two people on a blind date. Neither one of us knew what the other was thinking or wanted. I suggested that we head back to "my place" and just relax, she quickly agreed and I ever so proudly pulled into the parking lot of the school and we tried quietly taking the elevator to the room. The thoughts running through her head had to be similar to mine, what the hell were we doing? Sitting there we got to talking and that helped ease the tension quite a bit.

Patricia and I sat there and just held one another as she was now much looser and also telling me of what happened. After her one nightstand and a few fake hangouts with me she just went on to fuck numerous amounts of men and to my surprise a lot of them were much older than I. She went on to explain how she was with this married man for two months who had children and she decided to split once he agreed to leave his wife and family for her. She said it with an amount of pride that she probably never felt in her life. Her one and only talent were fucking men's lives up by constantly sucking their dicks and leaving them at their most vulnerable moments. I could just see the glow and life in her when going into detail about the endless amount of men she ruined. She also explained while keeping her legs spreaded wide open that all the money she had earned had come from these married men who felt their love lives were over and just wanted fresh young pussy to rejuvenate them once again. Black mailing was also another trick she often kept up her sleeve. It wasn't a surprise she was so good at this because it was something that had been done to her during her whole entire life and with years of constant abuse and neglect she had cleverly learned the game and was going to let her take it as far as she possibly could.

Most reasonable thinking human beings could see that she was going to take me for everything that I wasn't worth and leave me with less than I had before. But, when your life consists of waking up in the middle of the afternoon and cramming in school knowledge and trying to find your place in while drinking until you can't remember who or what you are it's hard to think straight or even crooked. None of that mattered because I was getting ready to pleasure a familiar face and that was something I wasn't use to. Going down on her made me feel like I was back where I belonged but in reality I was miles away.

After our event that evening was over with I did what I did best at night, and that reflecting on my life. This was something I did regularly before I went to sleep. It was my only sacred place in my mind that hadn't been corrupt with the outside world. Once again with her head resting on my chest I starred at the ceiling and I went back to my childhood.

In the midst of everything I just wanted to be a child again. I wanted my innocence back more than I wanted anything. With all the things I had done my life and mind were so corrupt that finding a way out now seemed almost hopeless. My mind kept drifting back and this time it led me to my six-birthday party. This one I had in my mind particular because I just got done the previous weekend watching it on video. My parents who I loved more than anything always recorded the birthday parties. I even miss those big old camcorders that everyone had. Back then that was the thing to have along with having a VCR put you ahead of the game. The whole thing was being taped in my backyard. The power rangers were all the rage in my life and getting that bicycle that was also a power ranger bike topped off what was a great birthday.

I remember the piñata that my father had hanging from the swing set where I spent many days. The grass was overly green and life was what it should always be and that was simple. My life was simple and I craved that simplicity ever since then. Nothing was hard and now the person I was or becoming was nothing like that innocent little boy that once existed. That person unfortunately, was just a memory and a memory that would be played in my head constantly.

It's funny how when you are young the only thing you dream about other than being a super hero is growing up and having big person responsibilities. Being older is something you spend so much time craving. I don't know who said it but I think the saying goes a little like youth is wasted on the young. That is one of the truest statements I have ever heard. Getting older only means getting closer to death and that means being real with everything and letting your imagination die also. Once the inner child inside of you dies then the man you worked so hard to become also slowly dies day by day. If you don't believe me just take a look around you. A child would never create a nuclear bomb and kill thousandths of innocent people. A child wouldn't put someone in a concentration camp and stand by as his or her families are brutally murdered. A child doesn't know racism and the deadly disease that it truly is.

Racism is something that will never go away. As long as there is someone out there that has different color skin that you or talks or walks different than you then we will have our world value known as racism. The adult that lives on the inside and outside of us is a killer. It's the all American killer. We let it sleep in our souls and it slowly becomes a part of our hearts and then it takes over the mind and as soon as you know it you are the very thing you spent your whole entire life hating and avoiding. Unfortunately, it is much too late for some of us to ever get our true sanity back.

Those are the type of things that run through my

mind constantly when I'm alone or just sitting in my bed with a girl's head resting on my chest. What did she truly see in me? I wondered that often, maybe too often. Was I just another person to have sex with and get out frustrations? Did I really mean anything to her at all? Was she trying to get back at me for all the shit that I had done to her? Possibly, but I just couldn't say no to her, she had me in a trance and that my friend is never good. Another thing that I desired about her was she made me feel like a man. When she would sit with me after sex it was as though I was finally doing what God put me on this earth to do. Maybe that was the real reason I never let her too far out of my reach.

While we were lying there I got another text and this time it was from James, he wanted to know how things were going with Patricia and me because he wouldn't just lend his car out to anyone let alone anyone with my reason. Quickly responding back I let him know that I got the present day monkey off of my back. That was one of our codes signaling that one of us got laid. Knowing that James wanted full out details and have his keys back to his car I told Patricia to stay at a friends house for the time being and that I would be home sometime to help her out. She reluctantly agreed and I walked her out of the room and out of the building. But something changed my mind; it was that I felt bad for her. She didn't want to go home or back to that same damn town and I didn't blame her at all. So like a gentleman I offered for her to stay the night and we would figure out the rest tomorrow.

The morning came and along with it came the awkwardness. This was expected but maybe not as much with a girl who had made her way around every house on the block. There was never a lost of romanticism with Patricia and I. We never did anything to make anyone think we were a couple; our dinners usually consisted of going to McDonald's and getting what we could get off the dollar menu. But all of that blandness was about to change.

Like I mentioned before James always had his own agendas and after getting a look at Patricia while she was all dolled up he decided there was money to be made from her. I couldn't have agreed more. Just like any product out there you want to sell a sure fire way to get your word out is through a female who isn't afraid to sell the product. After examining her with his eyes and feeling through a few places he had his mind made up that Patricia was going to make her way into the world by stripping. James was very good at persuasion. He knew from what I had told him about Patricia that her dreams always consisted of her being famous. All girls want to be famous and be some rich guy's woman and have their chance at getting on the tabloids. He explained so easily that being at a strip club meant that rich men have business meetings there and their eyes often get caught by a beautiful female dancer and the only thing it took was for one of those guys to really like her and they would become her sugar daddy. Of course he made her believe that this would be simple. James had all the right answers for her and she quickly became putty in his hands.

James knew that the relationship between her and I had to be broken up because I was heading to a lengthy stay in prison. James was a real friend and I knew that often times he did know best. Patricia and I even though would get involved in each other always tried to play it out that we both weren't into each other. We always put on a front in front of each other, even when she would open up feelings our relationship was always made out to be a fling where none of us really had any real interest in one another. Even though, I knew I had feelings for her.

James was always a step ahead of the game and here was a prime example, his best friend was a bong-hitting loser named Stan. Stan had lots of smarts but he never used them for good. He only used them to rip people off and steal things that didn't belong to him. Stan could make an easy fake identification card. To strip you had to be eighteen and Patricia was only sixteen. James cut a deal with her, he would give her this fake identification card so she could dance and this would lead to her making a lot of money because face it, all older men want a nice tight ass like hers to give them a lap dance and they will shell out the money for it, trust me I have made my way to strip clubs and the older you are the more you spend and shout. This money would allow her to live on her own and not have to rely on people back home and she wouldn't have to deal with her backstabbing friends that would intentionally hurt her on a day to day basis. In return, James would receive twenty five percent of the money she made. It was the perfect storm. Everyone made out nice, James could continue to live the life style he was accustomed to by getting loads of money from her plus the money his family would always put on his debit card. And Patricia finally had what she wanted and plus she had stars in her eyes that would eventually lead her into a life of more self-destruction.

Stan was the kind of guy you hated to have a conversation with because he always stood too close and his breath always had this rancid smell on it. The first conversation I had with him he spoke of how much money he had and the women he had lived to satisfy. Neither of these things I had any interest in hearing. He would say things like "Hey man this chick she was, uh, uh just fucking hot you know." I knew right from the start he would be someone I would have eventual trouble with. I didn't like him from the start because the first time I saw him he came up and put his arm around Patricia and said hey babe you gonna make a pretty damn good stripper. Just let me show you how to act and you will be fine. I can get you the proper treatment and get this thing on the ball.

Her eyes just lit up whenever he spoke and I could

tell that she was going to fall head over heels for this fucked up asshole. Patricia thought that she had just hit the big time with this stripper gig. James and Stan stood there with the biggest smiles on their face like they were some kind of clever con artists who made the deal of the century.

Patricia even had a partner in crime with this stunt of James and hers. The partner in crime was none other than Mia. This didn't come to as a surprise to me the least bit. Mia was always looking for attention and what better what to get attention than to slide around on a poll and spread your pussy for money. It got attention quickly and every other guy that lived in that boring ass town with a college. What else was there to do in a place like that other than go spend your money and help a poor girl pay her way through college? At least that's what Mia said she was doing and so does every female who goes and strips.

Mia jumped at the opportunity to show someone her naked body and oversized nipples she had on her chest that was just right. Mia thought of herself as the next Heidi Fleiss. She would make good money but it would only stay in the strip clubs and not some rich movie star's place for an evening. At least Mia had hopes and dreams.

Don't get me wrong at all I love strip clubs. I love that women will get up there and take off all of their clothes for money. It's essentially a billion dollar idea. It would be a total and flat out lie to say that I have never been to a strip club. Actually, I have attended them on three different occasions until that is I had friends there and that changed into frequent visiting. The girls as these clubs aren't like the way girls use to be. And by that I mean, their vaginas are always shaved and there is no hair down there or they have just barely anything down there. With little hair they think that they have something foreign and are being wild. Granted, a girl doesn't need to look like cousin it in that range especially when it is her career that consists of getting naked. But, what is wrong with all of these girls having little to absolutely no hair down south. God created you a certain way because he if in fact God is a he wanted you to be that way. So it always irritated me to a degree that a girl these days is well shaved in that region. The one positive thing about the gothic chick was that she wasn't pristine in her creation. I guess gothic girls feel they are completely different and have to be different down there also. But, they only do that because the believe life begins and ends with Marilyn Manson.

Before all of the shit went down for good at the strip club, James and I would take a leave for the weekend and headed back to his own hometown. Though James was living the high life at school he was dealing with a past that showed a different side to him than what others have come to know. He spent his early childhood years going back and forth to different foster homes and found it hard to stay put long enough to call someone mom and dad.

Where confidence was today use to be fear back then, on the way there he mentioned to me the struggles of going to school early on and how fighting everyday became second nature to survive. James was a fighter like none I have ever seen. He looked me in the eye and said when I was in junior high there was this girl that meant everything to me and I spent my entire time pushing her away every chance I could get. From book checking her to making fun of the way she dressed because her parents never had the money to spend on the useless shit that people think make someone have character. James had explained that he never knew how to treat someone who actually had a genuine interest in him so he shrugged it off like it meant nothing.

The moment finally arrived that we got to James place. The holes in the walls showed that fist was thrown into them more than a few times. The amount of dishes staked up in the sink screamed laziness and the dog food spreaded out on the floor gave the place a stench that almost made me vomit everything that I hadn't shit out in the past week.

His foster brother came out in was unusually quiet. I could barely understand a single thing that he said because he was very soft spoken. Not wanting to give anyone a reason to get on my case I didn't ask him to repeat anything, but instead nodded my head with a smile every time something was spoken. Neither the mom or dad was there but the pictures they had hung up on the wall where there weren't any holes showed that there were many different versions of the family.

James had shown me a bible where he had marked down all the psalms and verses that meant something special to him. In there contained a bunch of letters that he wrote to the girl in his class that he spent so much time thinking about but he never had the nerve send the letters to her. James wouldn't even tell me what the girl's name was. The brokenness and hurt in his eyes was undeniable. It was as though I could see through his soul and into all of his deepest thoughts and feelings.

In my mind, I couldn't wait to get out of the place and see the city. Our first stop was on main street at a strip club called looks that kill. James wanted to observe the women dancing there so he could give Patricia and Mia as many pointers as he could. I couldn't help but to notice all the women who different accents that worked that place. There were few white women there that talked sensible English.

The sign that was hanging up by the entrance made me a little nervous. It read, absolutely no Cumming in your pants. This made me real weary of getting a lap dance from any female that wasn't red blooded American. The fear of being premature in the V.I.P section was the very thought that kept me out of it. Like the way he always was, James had managed to make every single stripper in there fall all over him. They offered him free drinks and one woman even gave him a free lap dance.

After leaving the strip joint, we headed out to a regular bar and had ourselves a few drinks. There James would continue to tell me about his childhood and the troubles that went along with going to what felt like a hundred new schools. His drunkenness was getting too much and I had to walk with him back to his place.

The walk home preceded us with every homosexual slander and slur you could think of. Praying to God we wouldn't get killed proved successful as we managed to get back without a scratch. Lying on the couch in his living room I wondered if James ever wanted to track his real parents down and get the answers he really wanted. Just before he passed out in his bed, he looked at me and said, it's all about her man, and it's all about her.

The next morning left James nursing a hangover on the trip back to the university. Both of us weren't sure how to start off the conversation due to the honesty that was revealed the night before. But like any guy I jumped right into a conversation on sports. Particularly his favorite football, and if ESPN would constantly waste anymore time talking about Bret Favre and their love obsession with him. We both were sickened by the fact that the sports world desperately wants the Dallas Cowboys to be good every year.

Arriving to the university, we were greeted by Mia and Patricia who were more eager than a fat kid getting a shopping spree in a candy store about how their stripping venture would go down. I found Mia to be a little too desperate in all of her ideas and wants in life, but she made sure this time she would stay in the minds of people.

Mia who at times often was the life of the party and even she would jump on a pole and get a few guys aroused. I just found it as another desperate attempt at getting attention. Patricia and Mia suddenly became close friends and would do kinky stunts together on stage. Of course, James and I were now regulars at the club and sometimes would get free lap dances from them. But being the gentlemen we truly were we usually put down a twenty for the dance. The girls had to get by and this was their only source of income.

Once people on campus found out about Mia being a stripper they took on a different look and approach to her. The guys flirted a little more because they assumed she was easy and the girls looked down upon her. This even led to the diminishing relationship of her and Dani. Guys are so fucking dumb that at most times during the day I'm ashamed to be associated with them. In their tiny little minds they believe that a stripper will be easy to fuck and that when they talk sweet to you that means that she must have some interest in you. Many a men would return to their seats after a lap dance and say to their friend sitting next to them that hey dude, that chick stuck her tongue in my ear or she put her hand on my cock. Little do these so called men realize but this is a great strategy for the women. The more they constantly tease you back in those rooms the more and more you are likely to go back and continue to give them money just to fuck with your mind. And not your dick. These are the same guys that will go home and masturbate until it hurts for them to take a piss.

And once these measly games are over with and the men realize that there is no actual action to follow they form these nasty opinions of these girls to stroke their bruised ego. Sayings that go as followed. She's a fucking Skank. Dude, those girls are nasty as shit. Oh they mean the same girls they handed their paycheck over to so they could get a hard on and feel like they have actually gotten somewhere with the female race. I guess anything that boosts your confidence is worth doing.

The girls that spend their time looking down on other girls for making money for taking off their clothes are just in simple terms jealous. They're jealous that they either don't have the body to make money off of or they don't have the balls no pun intended to get up there and strut their stuff. Almost all females are she-wolfs. They can make another person feel like they are living their worse day and those they truly are what they are saying. Females only are what they think of other girls. It is a much easier way to deal with their own insecurities. And Mia was above all of them because she knew it and used it to her full advantage. This was something that really turned me on. It was surprising because Mia wasn't a girl that I found desirable just because she was always too damn annoying.

I kept a constant close eye on Patricia the whole time. She was what every older guy wanted to spend his money on. The innocent young girl that was not acceptably available because she is working at a strip joint. I think she really liked all of the attention brought to her. It was something she never in her life had the chance to feel. And that was accepted. Patricia was accepted here and no one was going to take her out of that environment. In her mind this was home and for once home meant somewhere she wanted to be. Men would shout her name out all the time and the money she was making off of them was mind blowing. James loved it too because he always got a cut from the profits. After all, he was responsible for making this happen for her. Patricia many a times would tell me how old men would blow their load in the back rooms while she was giving lap dances. She said that it disgusted her and that feeling it soaks through their pants was the grossest thing she had ever witnessed. I couldn't blame her one bit it was nasty as hell. No one wants to see Mr. Rodgers bust a nut.

One night in particular saw me at a vulnerable state. Patricia was having trouble with a client. This jerk wouldn't stop bothering her and taking no for an answer was something he wasn't use to. He just kept badgering her with no end in sight. This guy would throw his one-dollar bills on the stage and she would do a little dance like a monkey and take her little reward. Well, this guy wanted a lap dance and being the nice girl she was she gave it to him and he wanted it to go much further than that. I watched across the stage and she said no more. He yelled at her a few times and called her a word that you never call a girl and that was cunt. It is quite disrespectful. Feeling a fire rage inside of me I got up out of my seat, walked over and as soon as he grabbed her arm, I reached back and punched this asshole square in the teeth. I guess I didn't know my own strength because I knocked his fronts out and this old man dropped to the ground.

The bouncers who were late to begin with finally came over and they took me out back and beat the dog shit out of me. I ended up pissing blood for a week straight and the bruises left on my body didn't go away quick and made it extremely difficult for me to get out of bed. You would think that this would be the worse part of the experience. Unfortunately, it wasn't. The old man that I had knocked out was my English professor. Yes, the one class that I needed ever so badly to pass. Apparently, he was a regular there too and me hitting him in the face stopped him from going there for a while. He took his anger out on me. In the way he could hurt me the most and that was by failing me. He failed me on almost everything. Sure, he let me have the occasional D- from time to time. There was nothing for me to do about it. Telling the dean that this guy was a nasty pervert and was taking his anger out on me because I hit him at a strip club wasn't going to fly. Besides, I was only maintaining a c- for an average, so it wasn't so unbelievable that I would eventually fail. Once again, trying to do the right thing in life bit me in the ass. Not to mention the blood I pissed out.

Another detail that was eating me away was the amount of time James's friend Stan was spending with Patricia. I guess she truly was a whore and I meant nothing to her. I hated Stan with a passion. He was no good in every sense of the word. Stan was famous for his pot smoking and the drugs that he sold on a day-to-day basis. He was also fond of snorting cocaine. Always thinking he was smooth he bragged about how he snorted it pure. Calling it blow was his favorite term for the shit. Patricia was like a little kid, you could mold her anyway you wanted and this was one of the things that people could see miles away when looking at her and it always hurt her image. So experimenting with the drugs was something she didn't see as a big deal. It was something I hated but I could live with. What I couldn't live with was her fucking Stan. She owed me for doing what I did for her. If not for me, she would have never met Stan who eventually led her to making tremendous amounts of money and having her own life where she could stand on two feet. Plus, as far as I knew I was the only guy she was having sex with. She sure fooled me all right. The way they both tried to hide it was ridiculous and at the same time they would act like it wasn't a big deal.

When I got back Patricia's apartment that night I slowly went up the stairs hoping to not find what I had expected. Sure enough there they were there rolling around the living room fucking each other like they were meant to be. Acting like it didn't faze me at all I just sat down to which they stopped and drew out some more lines for each of them to snort. Trying to keep my mind off the pain and the betrayal I felt I kneeled down by the coffee table and joined them on their high. The cocaine was always pure, just the way Stan had always taught her to like it. Patricia while in her coked out state of mind looked up to me like she had no idea how she was making me feel and drew a few more lines out for her to take care of. But this time something was different. The feeling that I use to get from looking at her was starting to fade quickly. She wasn't the person that I use to think. Sadly, she was who everyone always accused her of being.

69

Even though Patricia was messed up pretty bad my eventual cold dark stare went right though her. Patricia loved the fact that she now knew she could hurt me. To me it was her plan right from the beginning to get under my skin and prove that she was underage that she could definitely hurt me. I had finally felt what she potentially felt her whole life and that was used. Somehow I knew this made us all another brick in the wall.

This wasn't something I felt comfortable confronting Stan on. I knew he was a snake in the grass and he knew how much I hated him. But, standing up for Patricia was something I vowed to never do again, and I meant that. Still though it hurt me. It hurt like hell.

Meanwhile, Stan and Patricia continued their love affair. Both of them thought they were doing it behind my back but the truth was they were so fucked up all the time they never realized how obvious they made it. Still though, I stood right by her side and could never bring myself to leave. Why did I feel such closeness to a female that did nothing but do me wrong. There's nothing like the feeling of loving something and never feeling the love back. It's like a death sentence to your heart. You feel so many emotions towards someone and the pleasure you think you have from them is nothing but a fantasy in your head. Every moment you spend with them you try beyond your means to make them into someone that can love you just a fraction of what you love them. Convincing yourself that one day you hope they will see what is best for them and be with you but in reality they will never see that and you're the one left to pick up the pieces of your own heart.

One thing everyone should always take with them is that you never trust another human being. Humans will only lie and rob from you. Just like when you're a child and you're convinced that something is real. The magic behind Santa Claus being real separates you from the adults. Not knowing that they know that it aren't real you buying into what you're told? What you don't understand is that the rest of your life you will be fed lies and you will just like when you were a child believe in them whole-heartedly.

Like I mentioned before, Patricia learned the game and how to play because she was initially beat at it her whole life. Her lies that you thought were truth will always come back to sting you. Sitting outside on steps of her apartment with a drink in hand she looked at me and asked will you always love me? At first I didn't know how to respond because neither one of us had ever used the word love before when referring to one another. Looking right back at her I responded, what do you mean? With tears forming in her eyes she looked back at me as though she was starring right through my soul and said I always thought you were the only one whoever really knew and understood me. I went over and put my arms around her feeling extremely good. Thinking to myself, she is finally becoming the person I wanted her to be for myself and this time things just might work out. Though, I should've known that something that would pack a punch was to follow. And it came with her saying to me while looking down I'm only sixteen.

The realization of how strange and deranged things had gotten was going past me at a hundred miles per hour. I knew that anything real was just a hope and that it couldn't ever really be. Lying out on the apartment I was just letting what had happen sunk in and all of those labels that could be thrown onto me. Instead though of numbing me with sleeping this time I drank until I couldn't remember anything. Before I drifted off into no mans land again I started realizing how much of an impact Patricia was making on my life and how I needed to get away from all of this but could never gather the strength of walking and going back to the life that I was living.

All the time away from Patricia I didn't feel any different than I did now. Actually, I felt much more alone now with her here than I did when she was gone. At least I had the fantasy play out in my mind that she was something she's not. Now though, it was all too clear who the real girl was. Still I wouldn't give up.

With her there and gone I spent my days swimming in meaningless pussy but it never fulfilled anything other than another senseless sexual desire. A man can achieve everything in life he wants and he can fuck as many women as he wants and make the money he only dreamt about as a kid but everything is left empty if he can't get the woman he loves. Without that, he spends time indulging himself in things that he thinks can take his mind away from it to a point where it won't affect him anymore, but in reality he is just running from the inevitable. The further and further he runs the more lost he becomes. Everyone around him may think that he has it made because it appears on the surface that he has no problems. But his heart is yearning for something he thought he once had and the harder fact to face is when he realized he never had it. That everything in his mind was just a game and a game that kept him sane long after he lost the battle.

Sometimes in life people change. They change the way they do things. They change the way they look and the way they perceive things. But, they never change they way people, events, and things make them feel. It might lessen or strengthen but certain emotions are always there to stay. You can run from everyone and anything but you can't run from yourself or from your past.

All of this was something I knew I needed to step back from and that was exactly what I did. The relationship between James and I had taken a hit because of Stan. James knew he was the one who introduced Stan to our group and Stan also knew how much Patricia meant to me. So our conversations for a while were kept to a minimum and nothing of substance was talked about for a few weeks. Everyone needed a break from one another. That was the God honest truth and a break was something that was granted. The first semester had finally ended and it was time to go back home and rejuvenate us for what was going to be an interesting second half of the year. My trips to the strip club stopped altogether and most of my contact with Mia was ended. My body was drained. I wasn't use to all of the stuff that was now going on in my life. The drinking and the girls had fogged up my mind and I couldn't see straight at all. It was as though I was suffocating. Living like you are in a Motley Crue tribute band was no longer fun for the time being. Also, I felt pretty upset at myself because I couldn't remember the last time I had a conversation with Dani.

As everyone was packing their things up and getting ready to head out it became official that Patricia and Stan were now a couple living in the same apartment building and sharing each other's profits. They were living large from the money she earned taking off her clothes and the money he earned from selling drugs.

Patricia knew that jealousy raged inside of me because of all of this. She knew that her being with Stan was something hard for me to deal with; it was, as though, she wanted to hurt me as hard as she possibly could. I didn't know how to deal with so the person I decided to hate the most was that fuck face Stan.

When I spoke of my hatred towards Stan, people and when I say people I mostly mean Patricia would say that I am just racist. The fact that Stan was black had nothing to do with me hating him. I hated him because he was a drug dealer; something I hated beyond anything in my life. He was a loser and never had anything positive to do. Hating him also stemmed from him being a thief and a chronic liar.

People can't hate black people anymore. That is something I have come to know. Black people can do whatever they please and if someone doesn't like it the reason must be because they are racist. The fact that they talk in a way that most people can't understand, or that they are lazy and expect the world to be handed to them has nothing to do with it. Why and how do people still talk about slavery as though people of today were responsible for it? It is something of the past that was wrong and extremely terrible. The white people of today aren't the white people of yesterday. Our society is extremely acceptable to many different kinds of people and had no role in those times. America isn't equal opportunity though. White people won't get hired because companies need black and Hispanics to make them look equal opportunity and leave the person who often times is more qualified for the position without a job. Where is the justice there? Why can't we get these benefits now? Sounds to me that America is still racist just this time against different people.

As I was getting into my car my phone was flooded with text messages from James trying to explain how he never intended on Patricia and Stan getting together and how he had hoped that this was something that wouldn't ruin our friendship. The messages kept on coming and coming until I got so tired of it that I turned off my phone and threw it in the backseat of the car.

In my head I knew that he wasn't responsible for all of this happening but it was easier to blame him and not myself for what had happened. For some reason it took quite a long time for me to accept James as a true friend again. I mean he had to know that Stan was the piece of shit he was and would not stop until he had my girlfriend. Then again, was she my girlfriend or was she another mistake that I had to find myself living with again?

Driving home I just blasted my radio and didn't think. Not thinking is what got me into the mess I was in, but this type of not thinking was healthy. The scenery around me might have been dead due to the winter but there was snow everywhere and it was pleasantly beautiful to look at. I got home and unloaded my things and lay on my bed where I starred at my Kiss posters and thought about how rapid my life was changing. Looking into the mirror I didn't see the same person who was there from years before. I didn't know exactly what I saw this time. It's scary when you look in a mirror and you can't put your finger on what you are seeing. Like it is just an image, one that doesn't resemble you anymore. No matter how many times you look in the mirror the same things just keeps staring back at you and it eats you up inside to know that you lost what you always admired in yourself. Not only did I lose what I always valued in myself but I lost what others valued as well. Things weren't the same anymore and they were never going to be the same again. Something that I had to come to grips with even if it felt like another knife being ripped through my heart.

Chapter 5
Into The Night

Driving through the cold abandon streets that I called my hometown, I found that there was nothing like the feeling of being home and being somewhere you could call your very own. It never had much appeal to me before or anyone that drove through it to get to their vacation spot. But it was mined nonetheless.

My old time best friend and I decided to head down to one of the million local bars and shoot pool while having a few drinks as long as we were there. After losing the first three games we both got to talk about our first semesters at our profound colleges. I decided to leave out many details about mine that included never telling anyone about the underage stripper that I managed to fall in and out an in love with. Or least I thought. My descriptive semester was limited to a few good lays and some memorable parties. Buying into everything I was saying he was congratulating me on my new ways of life.

He went on to tell me about the amount of women he had managed to pleasure and leave in the same twenty four hours. Knowing that the stories he was telling were a little stretched from the truth, I knew he was just trying to make me proud.

Finding my way over to the jukebox I took notice of the piece of shit place we were in. It hadn't been clean since its opening twenty years ago and the cobwebs that surrounded the place were a dime a dozen. The one thing that I admired about the joint was that it hadn't switched over to a high tech jukebox and it retained its original feel to it. Flipping through the classic music that crowded it, I came across a couple Bob Seger records and quickly put on Against the Wind.

Turning around to start up another game of pool, Leah and her new boyfriend came in and sat up by the bar and laughed the day away while getting drunk out of their minds. Continuing with my business I did everything I could not to look up at them and lose my cool. Wanting to beat the fuck out of the older douche bag she was with I thought of everyway I could to piss her off but she managed to beat me to the punch.

When her soon to be Vieira popping boyfriend got up to take a piss, Leah came over and asked how my underage love freak affair was going. Feeling I was being hit by a ton of bricks I responded with an immature an inaccurate answer with the words, at least her titties don't look like fruit roll ups. This led to a very hurtful, sad look over her face and she ran out of the place.

Leah was no longer my girlfriend so it wasn't my duty to chase after her snail trail. Sitting where she was at the bar her boyfriend came over with a fatherly attitude and asked where she had gotten to, I told him she went after a dick that could get hard in a matter of seconds and not hours with pills and heavy hand shakes. Looking at me like he was going to do something violent the old man just walked out of the place.

My old time friend Steve stood there with a huge smile while applauding my actions. I just looked at him and said sometimes you just need to do what you must do. Feeling like a total asshole after I verbally assaulted my first and real true love, I did what I had become accustomed to and that was drink and drink myself into oblivion. Steve tried easing my guilt by saying hey man she came after you, not the other way around. She asked for it, not you. Forget it man, she obviously wasn't worth it or she would have never left you for some Hugh Hefner wannabe. I just nodded and drank another beer while I remained at the palace that never saw any sunshine.

Before we knew it the day had turned into night and the joint was happening. People pilled into the bar to watch the local bands that were playing there that night. The bands were loud and great. The best part was they were playing good solid rock and roll.

Steve turned on his ladies man skills by flirting with every single woman there over the age of thirty. He got exactly what he wanted because many of them were all over him, placing their hands on his crotch and placing their phone numbers in his hands. Steve would latter take the night back to his place with one of the women there after he offered to take her out for breakfast after the show was over.

Even I thought that I was going to get lucky when I saw a tall gorgeous woman walk my way. She placed her hand on my shoulder and asked me, where did you get your shoes? Thinking to myself, this had to be a fucking joke. She responded, my husband has been looking around for those same pair of shoes for the last three months and he can't seem to find them anywhere. I told her I bought them at the local mall inside of footlocker. Though most of the time I would have felt embarrassed about the whole ordeal, this time I just laughed it off. People were starting to look at me quite different because I just couldn't stop laughing at the ridiculous question. Who the hell could spot a pair of shoes out of several hundred people at a bar in the dark?

Taking it upon myself to try to be useful, I helped the band pack up all of their gear and pack it into the truck. Congratulating them on a job well done, I walked myself back into the bar and sat there before it closed in twenty minutes. This time I felt like the looser because I was the only one in the place.

Too much of my surprise, the door to the joint opened

and I heard a voice saying we never got to take that dance. Looking behind me was Leah. She was just standing there with a hopeful look in her eye that I wouldn't be the asshole she had come to know lately. Turning around I said what dance would that be my lady. Leah smiled and sat by my side with my sad looking image and said the one you wanted me to take when you started playing Against the Wind.

Then I guess we should do it that then. Starting the song over and spending my last fifty cents, Leah and I danced to Bob Seger. Placing her head on my chest she spoke softly saying I didn't mean what I had said earlier. I just felt upset due to everything that had happened to us and finding out about your latest sexual adventure. I told her it wasn't any big deal and that I was the asshole.

Wanting to know why Leah was with another older man, I finally asked her that million-dollar question. Leah said that older men knew how to treat a girl right these days. The men of today don't know how to properly treat a woman and spend most of their time yelling out rude perverted marks and taking care of themselves. Older guys know the finer things in life and don't waste time that could be spent building a true and honest relationship.

Knowing in my mind that her answer was complete bullshit, I just agreed and finished out the dance. Lying through my teeth I told her that Patricia or Tricia was just a one-night stand that I didn't bother with after it was over. Hoping that if I acted like I didn't remember her name, Leah would believe my latest lie and not pursue any more questions about the subject.

Leah took my lie hook, line, and sinker. Afterwards, I walked her to her car and gave a quick kiss on the cheek and wished her all the best. She offered to take me home, knowing my current state of drunkenness.

The drive was a quiet one that led to me thanking her for all of her past love and commitment. She sighed and looked over to me saying it was good for what is was. Not caring that much these days I took it as a compliment. Little did I know it then, but that would the final time I saw Leah. She found the inner wild spirit inside of her and took off to California to be with her over forty sugar daddy. I never took it upon myself to see how it went or how far. It wouldn't have been too hard to find out but I thought it best to just hold on to what I use to have with her and move on. That proved to be one of my best decisions to this day.

Stumbling into the house the walk to my room was filled with falling into walls and hitting the ground before I managed to there. Finding the bed was a little easier.

Waking up in the morning was a minor disaster on my health. My stomach was a little more than upset and I was constantly thirsty. Thankfully remembering I had an appointment with the university's counselor, I gathered several bottles of water for the road, grabbed a shower and headed off to the death trap.

When I got there, I stayed in the vehicle a little longer to finish listening to my favorite Eddie Money song Two Tickets to Paradise. While standing outside in the cold I smoked my last cigarette for the day while debating whether or not I actually wanted to go inside and deal with the one hour session. Knowing it was in my best interest to follow through with the appointment and not have the counselor call home and alarm my parents who already had enough on their plates to deal with.

The waiting room looked like it hadn't been redone since the 1970's disco era and the two people waiting before looked like they did indeed help. Then again, who the hell was I to pass judgment on anyone? There was a guy sitting there that was fifty pounds overweight wearing blue sweat pants and spaghetti stained white sweater. He was just sitting there looking down at his phone like he actually had someone to text. Still he spent his entire time browsing through the whole thing.

There was a girl there that was very tall and had the skinniest legs I have ever seen. Her dirty blonde hair and tight jeans rounded out her image. Sighing every five minutes she finally got up and grabbed one of the magazines that had been sitting there for what I'm sure was forever. Woman's world magazine were scattered throughout the waiting room that dated back to early 2002. I wonder if everyone was obsessed with whom some Hollywood asshole was dating back then, as they seem to be now. The radio was set to an oldies station with Brandy (You're A Fine Girl) playing with the Faces Stay With Me following it.

After waiting for what seemed to be forever, my turn to go into the counselor's office had finally arrived. The only reason I was there was to please me worrisome mother. The counselor was a woman straight out of graduate school and couldn't have been over the age of thirty-two. She was gawky looking with a lazy eye. Instead of getting to the root of what was "wrong" with me, she just pried into my personal life to which I did nothing but make up disgusting lies that consisted of making her believe I had a collection of Asian ass porn and had a thing with girls that had pubic hair and liked to let their freak flag fly. The latter of my lies actually being true.

She went on to explain that I was a common case of cabin fever and that I tend to let the little things in life get too far in my mind to the point that I start to doubt the simplest things. Surprisingly enough, she was correct for the most part. She gave me a prescription for anti-depressants to which I threw away as soon as I got out of the session.

To say that the session didn't help would be a lie, but the amount of money I had to keep putting in my gas tank was killing me. So I stopped after one visit to her.

On the way back home, Steve and several other high school friends had called to see if I wanted to go out with them and have a good time. Still feeling the effects of the night before I decided to pass and just relax the rest of the day away. My mom had my entire bedroom cleaned when I got back and both my mother and father were overly caring and trying to hard to make me believe how much they loved me. I knew they loved me more than anything, but hearing it wasn't so bad. I just wanted them to know that I hadn't forgot their love for me so I stopped with my constant scary bullshit and decided I needed to get my shit together because the next stop for me might be in a asylum.

It was shocking that she hadn't said anything about the note that I had on my bed before I left. The note that I had stuck on my bedside told me that in a few weeks I would have to pick her up from rehab. I just hope the cops aren't waiting for me.

Chapter 6
Almost Human

The most satanic people in this world are the strongest believers in Christ. If you choose not to believe that then go right ahead, but it is the ugly truth. These people feel that God had abandoned them and there was essentially no hope left for them. The rejection from family and society is a wound that constantly has salt and vinegar dumped in it. On top of that, they develop this strong belief in Jesus Christ. Believing that he will solve their problems and just maybe all of this constant torture will go away. When reality starts to settle in after a few weeks or months and sometimes-even years' people develop hatred towards the Lord. People feel the one thing that was never going to turn their back on them and let them down just did so. That begins to hurt a lot more than anything they have ever expected. But, it doesn't take away their belief that he does in fact exist. The man and the religion just become something else they can hate and curse out. Just remember, God helps those who help themselves. Take that in anyway you want.

There is nothing in this world more powerful than money. What is even more troubling is the holder of that money. It runs everything in the world and there is no end in sight. Money controls the universe and it controls you and I every second of everyday. What happens when you love someone and they get sick? Love sure as hell isn't going to cure them. Money that pays for the best care will. What happens when you want the girl of your dreams and instead of taking her to a four star restaurant you take her to Burger

King? She will think you are a cheap bastard and move on the next guy that will splurge his money onto her. Even though, he may love her ten times as much as the guy who just wants a piece of ass and you would be there for her no matter, that doesn't matter. Because money shows class and style and we as a society are much more interested in that than anything that truly loves us.

Don't get caught up in true love or anything that says money isn't the most controlling thing on earth. Even God wants the hat passed around on Sundays. Money will also tear a family apart before other things. People would rather have you borrow their home lawn supplies, kitchen appliances, and even their own lover sometimes rather than give you ten dollars. Because that money possesses the true nature in all of us. And that is we are all money hungry demons. Each and every single one of us. Humans are natural born blood-sucking viruses. At the end of the day that is what we all are at the core of everything. No matter how much you help someone out in life and no matter how much you are there for them in their worst time of suffering if you need to get a few dollars from them that makes you equal on all levels. Money is the only reason why most of us get out of bed in the morning. We don't go to work and bust our ass or kiss someone else's ass Monday through Friday because we like it. No. We do it because we need to survive.

Animals need to kill other animals to survive and humans must make the most money they possibly can to survive. What is the most troubling about all of this shit are our church leaders. Take someone like Joel Osteen for example; he makes life out to be so easy and that being happy and healthy is such an easy task everything should follow his advice. Have you ever looked at the house and cars he drives? He is living way beyond his means and that MONEY would be better spent helping out people who are much less fortunate than him. Instead, he will rip you off and get you coming back for more. Robert Patterson would be someone to analyze but there is nothing to him other than he is one of the dumbest motherfuckers to ever walk the Christian earth. I'd rather watch gold on television that listens to his stupid ramblings. If God were to come down on earth this very second one of the first people he would send to hell would be that overconfident fuck.

I'd like to believe in a God or true love but it gets harder all the time to do. True love is something that may have never existed. People don't get married for true love, they get married because the person is financially stable and they have a good feeling they will be loyal to them. That isn't a bad reason to tie the knot; it's just the truth. Love is simply finding someone you can tolerate and be an attracted too. Most people don't marry or stay with the person they truly want to be with. And that is fine with most people because they let go of their childish crushes and move on with reality and what will better serve them. I'd learned all of this through finding the money for college and being with the cadaverous Patricia.

I knew it was best to let her go and spend my winter break finding a part time job. Patricia would tell me often times when she was drunk off her ass that her and I were the real deal. That we were what true love was all about. Once again, alcohol never fails.

During that month home I had the chance to pull myself together perhaps, in a way I wouldn't have been able to do while at school. The holiday season was officially here and Christmas was fast approaching. With that time away from school I dodged every attempt at drinking alcohol and getting fucked up on anything. It just was something that I didn't want to do but sometimes those strongholds don't hold up when you need them to the most.

I had spent the first week back watching my younger sister who slowly but steadily was growing up before my eyes and I didn't want her to. Having known the bullshit that life constantly throws upon you I didn't want her to go through all of it but I knew there wasn't a damn thing that I could do about it. She was going to grow up and go through everything just like I did and the people before us.

She was fascinated about asking me how college was and what I did up there all the time. Obviously not telling her the truth I made up simple white lies or simple black lies like how I spent my time studying and playing racquetball in my spare time. I let her know how much an education was worth and that she needed to pursue a degree when it came time for her to graduate high school. Thank god she wasn't in high school yet.

I thought it ironic how I was telling her how much good college could do for you when I knew it wasn't doing a damn thing for me. I had turned into my parents and the teachers who always expressed how good something is and how much needed it is but know deep inside that they are just fulfilling your head with a bunch of bullshit.

As the weeks went by so did the usual familial drama that goes along with everything in life. The same old scenarios rear their ugly head and this time I didn't care the least bit. It wasn't something that unsettled me. To me it was a way of life that I had become accustomed to. Never having money and depression were the usual looming feelings in the air. So I did what I could to avoid them and that was taken up a part time job. Working at a tobacco place was easy, the hours were decent, but the boss was a bitch. Any time you have to work for a woman, the end result usually is quitting or being fired because women are terrible to work for. And when I say women are terrible to work for I mean older women. They think that the world owes them something. Older women are man-hating monsters. Not all of them are like that just most of them.

To get the job, I had to lie through my teeth. Telling

them that I wasn't a college student and I was trying to figure things out and just needed a part time job to keep me busy and my options open. The store wanted an employee that wouldn't within a month leave and go back to college. So here I was, a twenty year old that was out of high school and wasn't doing shit with his life but working at a tobacco outlet. That was my reputation at the store. The attitude the customers and employees took upon me. The she wolf that I worked for spent her whole time while I was there doing nothing but harassing me. Working a register and some lottery machine wasn't a tough task but damn when you made a mistake she sure as hell would let you know and this followed by the customer getting pissed off and showing me that they too were disappointed. It wasn't a big deal to me because lately the only thing I was doing was letting others down.

I remember the boss yelling at me constantly. She would say demeaning things like I can kick your ass. I hope you know that. My son is much bigger and capable at this job then you. What do you plan on doing for the rest of your life? Do you always have your head lodged in your own ass? These remarks pissed me off tremendously. I wanted to for the first time in my life beat a woman. But, I didn't. Who fucking cares that her son could do the job better than me? And I don't think she would have gotten too far kicking my ass either. The most excitement that I got from the day was taking the trash out. The ten second walk to the dumpster was filled was fun.

Women who are in control have this thing in their mind that they have to be a bitch to everyone. They assume that people just don't respect them and that their job is to let everyone know who the real boss is. Every time I had to work for a woman the woman was always in a bad mood. Women can be such bitches at times. I have a hard time deciding if I love them or have an extreme passionate hate for them. The only thing recently that I liked was their ability to fulfill my needs and lately now with Patricia gone that wasn't happening either.

On top of the boss being a bitch, I had to deal with the endless impatient customers. This one asshole in particular was an older man probably in his late fifties and he was from New York. I guess that meant that he was tough. This guy would spend endless amounts of money of lottery tickets everyday and he apparently never won. His accent was so hard to understand that trying to make out what he was saying was a job in itself. So thinking I was getting his numbers right, I pushed them into the machine. Apparently, they were the wrong numbers and this little New York man just went fucking ape shit. Screaming at me and telling me how pissed he was and I was lucky. Lucky for what? Lucky for what? Lucky for what? I guess I was lucky that he didn't decide to hurt me. That was what he was trying to convey to me. Holding back my true feelings I stood there for as long as I could before snapping. I would have permanently damaged this old fuck. I just wanted to grab him, throw him over the counter and beat the shit out of his pansy New York ass. Fuck New York and the assholes they produce that think because they come from a big city that it makes them tough.

Well I finally did lose my temper and told him to take his loud mouth ass outside and leave before I threw him through the door. Stunned, the old man just decided to leave. That didn't set well with the boss and once again someone was chewing my ass out. I hated the job. I hated waking up and having to see this woman's face. So once I decided that I had enough, I made sure to let it well known.

The day came that I had to run the store by myself. Tired of all the customers and their low life bullshit, I tried to be as nice as possible. I had my own key to open up with, but the great woman boss never gave me the password to open up the register. Customers were lining up by the dozen and I was panicking ever so badly. Deciding that I finally had enough I told all the customers to come back in an hour and everything will be taken care of. I even told them that the boss gave me permission to give discounts because of all the trouble they have had to endure while I was working. This helps ease the anger quite a bit with the customers. So once the store was clear, I decided to close everything down seven hours before closing. I left all the money scattered on her desk and to top things off I put a sign outside the door saying be back after lunch. And that was the end of my stay at tobacco discount.

Upon getting into the house, I checked the mailbox to find a letter addressed to me. It was from Patricia. Deciding that it would be better to open this in my own room and read it lying down I just tucked it in my pocket. Lying on my bed I thought to myself, when does this ever end? She was finally I thought out of my life and now she wants to write me a letter. What the hell could she possibly want? I knew her too well to think that she was going to give me something. But, you just never know.

I began reading the letter that began like this:
Lately I have been feeling a little upset about how things happened between us. I think that if given the proper opportunity we could be together and make this relationship work. Being with Stan started out ever so nicely as he was always nice and sharing with me all that he owns. He would say things and do things to make me feel like I was worth having. Something you never did. You never showed me that you wanted me. I always felt like I was a nuisance in your life and that you were content on having casual sex with me. That doesn't set well with me and that's now what I want from you or anyone. Just like you and everyone else, I'm a person. I'm a person with emotions and feelings and desires in life. People often times count me out and that hurts. There's

so much I could offer to another person and to the world in general. The reason you are reading this letter is because I am pregnant. Yes, I'm pregnant and I don't know how to deal with this. This wasn't something that I had planned and it wasn't something that I wanted. Scared doesn't even begin to explain how I feel right now. To make things even more complicated, the father is not with me right now. The father hasn't been a part of my life in close to month. The father is you. I think we need to talk. Call me.

Love, Patricia.

Patricia explained that she was now three months pregnant and she couldn't afford her place anymore. This was because Stan had taken off for good and being pregnant means not being able to swing around a poll for money.

My heart felt like it just fell out of my chest. Astonished and in disbelief is what I was in. What was I to make out of all of this? Not only did I get a girl pregnant, I got an underage girl pregnant. There was something about this letter that I questioned without end and that was I wasn't the father. There was no way I could have been the father. More than likely, Stan was the father and he must have split which means she put the weight on me knowing I was fool enough to go along with such bullshit. I didn't believe her for a second and getting to the bottom of this was something I had to do.

Without giving much warning I drove back to her apartment. When I got there Patricia was sitting in front of the television. As soon as she opened the door she decided to hug me. Acting as though nothing had happened between us and things were just going to go back to normal. The thing is, nothing was ever normal between us. We were always strangers to one another and the only time we had ever connected was when we were in the bedroom or getting drunk. And that isn't a reason to continue a relationship. A relationship must be built on trust, love, and commitment.

Something she had no clue of.

Another thing I had started to notice about Patricia was her looks were changing. I don't mean that she was maturing either. Her face was pale and her body was thin and worn. Even if she wasn't pregnant there was no way any strip club was going to hire her. She now looked as though she had the body of a twelve-year-old boy. I asked her what she had been doing with all the money she was making. This girl was making two grand a week and living in an upstairs apartment that was essentially dirt-cheap. Where did all of that money go?

Patricia stood there giving me one bullshit answer after another until it was clear to me where her money was going. She had become a drug addict. This made me furious. Losing my temper I started screaming and breaking things in the apartment. Asking how the fuck did you let this happen to you? How reckless of her to let herself get to the point of becoming an addict. I guess the hardest pill to swallow was that she was not only an addict but she was a heroin addict. What did this mean for our unborn child? Was the baby going to come out all fucked up because of her carelessness?

She sat there on the couch and went into detail of how things spiraled out of control for her. Also, I should have known that Stan was behind it all. He introduced it to her. Patricia explained how people were looking for Stan and he had to leave for good. Upon leaving, he had taken all the money with him and only had the courage to leave her a note. Was it my responsibility to pick up the pieces? Now with him gone, her pregnant, and being an addict I got the gory details of her addiction.

The rest of the nights at the club consisted of more fucking from Stan and for myself I stayed comfortably numb. This time I had started using more than cocaine. The rush and feeling I got from cocaine was priceless. It was like a good friend or somewhere there are guys with a fetish for this but the owners at the strip club weren't going to have a baby being born on their elegant stage.

One of the first things out of my mouth was I needed to have a DNA test to know for sure that this child was in fact mine. This made her cry her eyes out. Yelling at me, explaining how I corrupted her and that this was my entire fault. She even threatened to go to the police and have me thrown in jail. My head was spinning one hundred miles per hour and I just wanted this shit to end. To be honest, I didn't want the damn baby. No part of me wanted to be a father and I literally prayed to God that it wasn't my child. How was I ever going to give this child a home? I had no income and this meant me dropping out of college. That was the last thing I wanted to do. My plan in life had always been getting a college degree and getting a job that I wanted to do and make money. Nowhere in there I wanted to screw and underage girl and have a child. To top it off, I didn't want to go to prison. I was stuck between a rock and hard place with no possible way out.

Looking at Patricia telling me her story I was just in disbelief. This wasn't the same girl I first met. Not only was her life spinning out of control, it was sucking me in and I couldn't breathe. The situation suffocated me. I knew I had to get her into a rehab. That was the first step to take in all of this. But first, I was more concerned about whether or not the child she was carrying inside of her was mine or not. That question haunted me every time I needed to go to sleep. Patricia wasn't the girl I wanted to have children to and she wasn't the girl I wanted to spend the rest of my life with. Life as I knew it was changing and it was changing rapidly.

She went on to give me the details of her time away from me. The first time I ever-used heroin it was like hell. I vomited a shit load of times and I thought I was going to die. It was easy to convince myself that I would never try something to awful again. But it slowly became something

I couldn't live without. It was like a twisted love affair that stimulated everything inside of me. Just like being with Stan, I loved him but I was too young for him and he was nothing but trouble. There was something about him that I just couldn't live without and the more I was with him the more my life was in jeopardy. This friend was what heroin did for me.

The anger and rage I had for Stan was to the extreme. He had been doing heroin two weeks before I had ever witnessed it. How dare he keep something from me that I let myself indulge in? Moving on from that incident from which I didn't speak to him for two weeks we quickly after that made up. It was easy to make up when the only thing starting to link you to someone is a drug. We continued our days in a purple haze that was much of a blur. The stay in the clubs was the start of something that both of us would have to live with until the day we die.

We would always take drives to his friend's house to get what we needed. Considering this man had every kind of drug available at his place and enough drugs for everyone to enjoy I guess this was his way of letting me know he was the one in charge. On the car ride there everything from that past trip was flying a million miles per hour through my head. Questions that were reoccurring thoughts in my head were once again the idea of how did this all happen? How do I make it stop? I didn't want to be an addict and I never wanted to be a mother. Somewhere in my life I became both of them. I couldn't stop abusing myself with drugs. It was the only way I knew how to deal with anything. When a problem came up all I had to do was either snort lines of coke or stick a needle in my arm. This was ironic because growing up I hated the site of needles and blood alike. The sense of euphoria was extreme. My skin started getting a warm flushing feeling and everything in my mind seemed clouded.

The next morning when all of the tension had begun to wear down, we packed all of her things and checked her into the local drug and alcohol rehabilitation center. When I dropped her off, I hugged her and left. She could only contact me two weeks after she was in. At least, she was going to get the help she needed and the baby in her was going to get help. I hoped that anyway.

When I left her I had the emptiest feeling a human could have for himself or herself. Driving away I had to pull of to the side of the road. I got out of my car and cried my eyes out constantly. I don't think I ever wept that hard in my life. Right before my eyes, my life was crumbling down and every time I tried improving it something came along and kicked me right down. I didn't know if I was going to get out of this being fine or not. Now, I supposedly had a child on the way. While I was crying, I dropped to my knees and began to pray to God to let things work out and that I would straighten out my life. Just give me this chance.

During her time away, I received letters from Patricia constantly. They sounded psychotic and it was hard to read them. She went in great detail about how terrible things were and how I needed to get her out of there. I knew the best thing for her was to stay there so I decided after awhile not to read the letters because they only hurt me inside and I couldn't take the pain. Patricia took on extra baggage that I never knew about. When she was little she sister killed herself because she was heart broken over a guy. Patricia's sister was only sixteen at the time and was nine years older than her when she died. This didn't leave her with many memories, but the heartache never left and it was expressed strongly when she wrote me. Her letters consisted of this.

When you look back on your life do you see regrets or fulfilled promises? You know when I was just a little girl and my father left I walked into my mother's room because she was crying. I put my arms around her and said mommy

I love you. She looked at me and pulled me in close and said to me you can be anything in this world you want to be. If you have visions and dreams you need to have the courage to pursue them because when you dreams and hopes die so do you.

Driving out of there my intentions was to get clean and to stay that way. I never imagined the battle that would unfold for me as I tried to do this. That drive from my apartment was perhaps the most refreshing drive I ever took in my life. Cruising along I tried to the best of my ability to breathe in the fresh air around me; this is a hard task to pull off when you're struggling to keep your sanity. On the drive I just kept looking down at my cell phone trying to decide if I should give Stan a call. Knowing damn well that doing so would only bring me trouble that I had no more room for in life. On top of that, I was only sixteen so how long could I keep going on with this until my luck ran out?

I didn't know what was to occur in my life at that time. I never knew I would lose myself and I would turn out to have a life in organized crime and be a drug addict. Look at my pictures when I was just a kid. You don't see someone who had anger and killing in her eye; you see someone who is just as innocent and pure as God's hands. Now what has happened to me? I had to get this monkey off of my back. Trying to get myself to recovery I kept a journal so if I made it through all of this I would have a quick reminder what life was then before I decided to do it all over again.

Going through all of her letters I decided that I didn't want to see her journal. Sometimes you have to respect others privacy and let things go unknown. The rest of the time when she was gone was like a haze. Trying to figure out just whom I was and what I now wanted to accomplish in life. If this child was indeed mine then I needed to start shaping my life different. Which person would I let myself be?

Every time I look in the mirror I see a different face.

There are so many faces looking back at times I don't know which one is really me. The mirror shows all of my sides good and bad. The college student, the young man, the father, the obsessed lover. Sometimes I see a punk and someone who took advantage of someone that I had no business ever coming into contact with. Regardless, I had to soon choose which one of those faces was to stay and which ones were to go. A decision that would indeed take some time and one that unfortunately needed to be made soon.

I wondered about Patricia that whole entire time. She wasn't no longer the girl who I had gathered strong feelings for. I wasn't sure that I was capable of loving her the way a person needed to be loved. There were so many things that had occurred between the two of us that living a normal life together now finally seemed ridiculous.

Two weeks were up and she was now allowed to use the phone for calls. She called me every chance she got and she would go on and on about how much better she was feeling. I guess the withdrawals were over and now she was t focus on staying away from Satan. This task would be no easy one at all. Saying no can be the hardest thing in the world to accomplish. Temptation is truly at the root of all sin.

It is a voice in your head that will never let you go. The more and more you try driving it away from you the more and more it will attack your mind. In many ways temptation to me is a game with your mind. It's a game that will take you a lifetime to win. Many will never win the game and they will spend their days lost and trying to find themselves. One of the secret weapons of temptation is time. It has no sense of meaning. Time means nothing to temptation making it an almost unbeatable monster. It is more than a game once you get older. It goes from a game to a life style for everyone. You either put a lid on it to keep it from overflowing or it spills all over and ruins you. Once it overflows, keeping it still will be the hardest thing you ever have to do. The mess it leaves is one that stains your soul and picks apart your brain. Temptation lies in everything we do and drugs is just one of its many forms.

With two weeks under her belt Patricia had just two weeks left. I knew that those two weeks were too short and more counseling would be needed. Addiction is a life long battle, one that should never be taken lightly. But all too often it is.

Christmas finally came and it was a bleak one at that. The only thing on my mind was the baby and how and if we were going to make it. Not telling anyone of what was going on in my life was a killer. How could I let my parents know that life as I knew it was over and another form of myself was about to step in? Also, I didn't want to ruin the holiday season for anyone. Especially my sister who had spent the last month or so just waiting for me to come home an have an actual family event. Sitting at the table my heart felt light that it seemed it was stuck in my throat. I couldn't figure out what I was going to do. My sister had the usual happy glow that a kid who is clueless about the world had, my father sat there like this was the last place in the world he wanted to be, and my mother did all that she could without speaking her mind in the middle of that households annual catastrophe.

I wondered if both of them could see through me like I could see through them or were they just as blind to everything as everyone else seemed to be. As much as it did matter it wasn't the important issue at the moment. I felt as though this was how everything would be and I couldn't do a fucking thing to change it.

This was something that only I was going to figure out. But the question that still haunted me was the first thing that I asked Patricia when I arrived at her apartment just weeks ago and that was, is the child mine? Of course, she wanted it to be mine. Patricia desperately wanted it to be mine. More than anything, she needed it to be mine.

While Patricia was away I was left alone. I didn't want to be left alone. Being alone means watching Internet porn and jerking off a few times a day. Masturbating also helped take some tension off of my mind. The scary feelings of being a father and having to spend my life with a woman I had only imagined loving was scary as hell. All of this led to me giving two of my hometown friends a call and having some fun.

Mark and Ray were two people always looking to have fun and have fun is what we did. Traveling back to my college town we decided to hit up the local strip club where all hell had broken loose just little over a month ago and where Patricia's life took another turn for the worse. One of my least favorite people but one of my most favorite dancers was there. That was Mia.

I showed up to the club drunk out of my mind, in fact I vomited my brains out three times before we entered the club. Sitting down at the table where I spent many nights gathering fantasies and material to latter on jerk off too was several dancers teasing us. One of the girls had the largest boobs I had ever seen in my life. In fact, they were so large that it grossed me out. Those tits had stretch marks all over them. When she put them in my face the feeling was extremely soft and awkward. In my entire life I never felt boobs that were so offensive in my life. To top things off the girl had bucked teeth. That's never a turn on. Not for me, not for you, and not for the catholic priest who enjoys fondling little boys.

After waiting several minutes, Mia finally made her way over where she greeted me by grabbing my cock. She grabbed it in a way that I got instantly hard. Giving her a few ones she ever so pleasantly shoved her tits in my face. While she was dancing, her eyes were fixed on me and she strutting everything god gave her to the Ac/Dc song You Shook Me

All Night Long. For once it was nice to hear a girl take off her clothes to a pure kick your teeth down your throat rock and roll song. I had grown tired of hearing the shitty sound of rap and hip-hop blare through those fucking speakers. No girl could pick a cool song to take off her clothes to anymore. There was nothing to be desired about the song and of course it was something that I enjoyed you could bet your sweet ass that no one else enjoyed it. That song was something that was summing everything about this school year up for me.

This led to me wanting more and wanting it now. She whispered in my ear softly to go in the back from with her and that is exactly what I did. Going back there, her song started playing and in seconds she was completely naked. On my leg, I could feel her grinding hard and making moaning noises that I thought were fake. Strippers are not stupid and they know how to fuck with your minds just as good as they can fuck with your dicks. But, something was different. When she got up my pants were wet and the wetness came from Mia Cumming on my favorite pair of jeans. The look in her eyes said let's fuck and for the first time in close to a month I got pleasured the way God intended.

What I liked the most about Mia was that she was Puerto Rican. Puerto Rican girls are some of the sexiest females in the world. They have this look and sway to him or her that is matched by no one. Every guy at some point in life wants to be with a Puerto Rican woman. And I was finally getting that chance. Some Puerto Rican girls were born to fuck and Mia was in that elite category.

It was strange because my entire life I had never received attention from a Hispanic or black girl. They never seemed to know I was there and for the most part I didn't care because I hadn't wanted anything from them. That was up until this point.

Mia had one of those vaginas that needed to be opened up. Even when she was naked you couldn't get the real deal. So to get where I needed to be, I spread opened her pussy lips and got to hump. Penetrating and feeling her hot warm breathe on my neck I was afraid that I was going to bust a nut way too soon. Fortunately for me I didn't do a thing. I thought it might be nice to lick her boobs and with those glorious objects bouncing up and down I sucked on each of her nipples and motor boated the rest of the way. Fucking Mia felt like coming home. There was no better feeling that sensation of Gods creation fucking you in all the right ways.

Afterwards, I thought it to be a nice gesture so I gave her forty dollars and told her that it was well appreciated. My friends were having the time of their life also watching the girls on stage but it was time to go. Once our stay at the club was over we moved the night at Marks house.

There we continued to drink our problems away and talk trash on just about everyone we could think of. This led to exploring his dad's box of pornography hidden under the computer. Though we were too old to be so juvenile I thought it fun to pry into his old mans life. There were so many fetishes DVDs in there that you would have thought his dad had never been laid. I never knew anyone to be into such crazy shit. It also made me wonder if his mom did what his old man was into. Something inside of me said she didn't because then he would have no use for such material being hidden. Maybe he was afraid to explore with her on those certain levels. If so that's sad. It wouldn't have been too much of a surprise because his dad was remarried for the third time and had only been married for three to four years I believe.

All of this fun for the night was a relief off of my mind. But, things were getting out of hand with Patricia though. She decided to send me her journal that was kept during her dark times as she called it. One of my fears was that she was going insane and there was nothing I could do to stop it. The journals were filled with entries where things were happening that I couldn't follow. Apparently, she had no idea of what was real during those days and what was fabrication of the mind. Patricia's world was right before my eyes in these journals.

The entries were horrific and they started out with her numbering the days. I guess the first nine days were the worse for her. I hope they were because I couldn't imagine reading anything that was more startling than this.

Day One- Today is the first day that I am attempting to go without any smack. That shit is only poison and I need to keep telling myself this if I want to stay clean. It hasn't been so bad. My thoughts and I are just sitting in bed holding each other. We are talking about our future like we did when we were in high school. When I finally kick this shit we will start a family and move away from here. I think I will take my money and run. She likes the idea of staying in the Philippines. That is just fine with me I guess.

Day Two- The feeling of needing this shit is again taking over me just a little. At night I seem to sweat a lot. The hallucinations haven't been here in awhile and thank god for that. I have just been walking around thinking about being able to breathe fresh air again. It will be like getting a new body. The amount of food I have been eating has also increased. I think I can do this. It hasn't been as bad as it was before trying to quick. Maybe this time I can actually do it. But without dope I will be able to make much more of a profit. It won't be a junkie making a deal with another junkie as much as it will be a professional ripping off a junkie and turning a profit like I use to.

Day Three- Everyone says I am starting to look a little bit better. I don't feel that way. I have spent the last three hours running to the bathroom and throwing up. My skin is getting that itchy feeling again. What the hell am I going to do? I am starting to hear noises and I can't tell if the rest of the underground world knows that I am cracking at the seams or if I am just taking some time away to plan my next move. The sweats are also getting a lot worse. The bed sheets have been changed three different times. My arms don't even look like arms. The skin is changing colors. The nurse tells me that I am just imaging things but I don't know anymore. When trying to stand I fell flat on my face. What will tomorrow have in store for me?

Day Four- This day is only getting worse. All firearms in at this place have been kept out of my reach. Am I locked into this room or can't I seem to find a way out. What the fuck? I gave the nurse the beating of her life. Throwing her to the ground I continuously hit her until I saw my favorite color red. Then I stopped. Now she isn't even coming into the bedroom. My whole entire body is shaking and I can't stop. Did I even wake up today? Did I ever hurt her? I can't tell what is real and what is a lie? I believe I just watched the bedroom floor turn into the ceiling. Vomit is everywhere. Someone needs to clean this shit up.

Day Five- did the past couple of days even happen? No one will tell me. Where is my help? Where are my eyes? I can't see, what is happening to me. Sweat is everywhere. Where is this all coming from? When I sleep I see my father and I going for a walk and talking about things. He just keeps on smiling saying Patricia one of these days you will be able to accomplish whatever you want. The world is yours don't let it pass you by. Daddy. Daddy please doesn't go come back and hold me. I am just a scared little girl. Please hold me and tell me everything will be just fine. Dad. Wakening up can be the worse experience for some. The nurse is standing there trying to calm me down. Where is her face? I don't see anything. Why can't anyone hear me scream? This is hell.

Day Six- I can still hear my sister yelling come on Patricia; let's go for a bike ride. She isn't there. She isn't there. Is my mom making dinner? I hope so because I haven't had a homemade meal in forever. What the fuck? Nothing exists. Now I am in a plain white room and no one is around. Where is the exit? There is no way out. HELP!!! HELP!!!! No one can hear me. There is that little child again. Did I give birth? She didn't do anything but have a father that was full of crime. I killed him and watched him die. What have I done? Nurse. Nurse, where are you? I need you honey. Sweetheart. The nurse is here again and still I see no face. What the fuck there are men all around me and I can't see again. HELP!!!! Someone please help me.

Day Seven- I woke up and no one is here. I am back in this bedroom and the walls are gone. It is raining and I can still see Stan and all of the abuse I endured. It wasn't an innocent beating either. The nurse is here again. She is here and the ceiling has also disappeared. For the first time it's what I think is years now I see myself. I look like hell. Why is my face all is bandaged up? My eyes are black and blue and my lip is cut open pretty bad. That bandaged on my head makes me not even want to think what happened. Did I do this to myself? What is wrong with me Lord? What is wrong with me? Why would I do something so horrific? And for the first time in awhile I looked at my skin and it isn't there and neither is my bones. But I can still see myself. How does that even make any sense? Am I dead? Fucking heroin it ruins people's lives. Look at the monster I have become. My empire; where is it? Am I still on top of my game?

Day Eight- My baby's face is like an image that I

can't get out of my mind. He is there with me throwing that football and the next moment we are in the bedroom talking about our hopes and dreams. He can't be dead he is right here standing in front of me. Is he dead? Oh Why am I seeing this? Can you hear me? Can you hear me? Why can't anyone hear me? Why doesn't anyone hear me? How did my eyes become torn out? I am sweating my whole entire body off. There isn't nothing left of me. And the room is spinning out of control. Is this really happening? Please someone help me? This is it I am dying. My skin is pealing off and I there am scratch all over my bones. Why can't I stop scratching everywhere? And the smell of anything is making me vomit. Where is my soul? I think I just saw it leave my body and out the non-existent window. My whole entire body is cramping up. The vomit is all over the bed now. I haven't eaten anything in days why am I vomiting so much. My nose feels as though it is coming off of my face. The snot and blood is just gushing out everywhere. Stop. Please stop. I must be dying because on top of everything else I have been shitting constantly and it feels as though I have been lying in it forever.

Day Nine- I don't know what it feels like to feel anymore. I have lost all sense of what is right and wrong and I have lost all sense of anything. As it turns out I had to be committed to a hospital. And today I get to leave. This journal has been by my side this whole time and I didn't even know it. All of that shit that I thought was happening apparently was all in my mind. I think that is bullshit. I know I saw and felt everything. Oh yea my face is bandage up because I did beat myself pretty bad. I'm sorry for everything. I loved you more than anything. I finally get to go home. Even though I have been clean for ten days I will have a desire for it for quite some time. Please lord helps me stay off of this shit.

Well it just goes to show
Things are not what they seem
Please, sister morphine, turn my nightmares into dreams
Oh, cant you see I'm fading fast?
And that this shot will be my last

Sweet cousin cocaine, lay your cool cool hand on my head
Ah, come on, sister morphine, you better make up my bed
cause you know and I know in the morning Ill be dead
Yeah, and you can sit around, yeah and you can watch
all the clean white sheets stained red.
-    The Rolling Stones-

Not knowing what to think or do I just took these journals and stored them away in a closet for hopefully no one to see. I spent so much time wondering and hoping if Patricia was going to be the girl without all of that psychotic shit or be insane the rest of her life. Her addiction to drugs was one that I never knew had so much power. In these books I read and felt how bad a person can get and the struggles that losing you can bring. In every aspect possible Patricia had lost herself. What was more troubling was that I myself was losing my control and hold on life. Something I never imagines possible. Was I the next one to completely crack and hit rock bottom?

That night I got home and found myself having to crawl through my bedroom window to get in. The doors were locked in it was five in the morning. I lay on my bed and in a matter of no time my eyes were closed and once again my mind was off to dreaming.

This time I can remember it being cold outside and school was just closed for the day due to snow. Climbing out of my bed and looking out the window in amazement. The snow was so pristine looking and it had a crystal glare hitting the surface. Running out into the living room and seeing my mom awake, she had already begun to make me some hot chocolate. The house was nice and warm because we had a fire going and life to me couldn't get any better.

Mom and I were watching her favorite old show Gilligan's Island. Nick at Night was showing reruns and we would gather around the television and watch these strange episodes that I loved with no end. The time came that I got to go outside in the snow. I was alone but I liked it that way. Not wanting anyone around to ruin my imagination. Our dog loved the snow and she was running around all crazy and happy. Her and I played around in the snow and wrestled. Walking and lying anywhere in the yard and looking at the sky seemed almost perfect. The gray sky was heavenly looking and innocence was everywhere to be found. Nothing corrupt was going on and the only thing on my mind was I hoping that tomorrow could follow today along with a possible cancellation for school again or a delay to the start. Everywhere in the neighborhood was safe to go. Everyone was inside for the day and the streets were covered still in snow and life was once again the way it should be. Easy.

Chapter 7
Rip it Out

It was a Thursday morning, the last week of my winter break and I was driving to pick up Patricia from her stint in rehab. The drive there was tough to do considering everything that was occurring between us would be awkward for any other couple except that it was quite normal for us. If a couple was what we truly were. That part was never decided between Patricia and me. Though it was an interesting roller coaster, it was one that was starting to make me feel sick inside.

With a million and one thoughts running through my mind I wondered if this time would truly change anything and it left me with a feeling of uncertainty and uneasiness. But that's how my usual daily feelings were now. I hated those rehab centers. The way the people working there look at you, it makes me want to shoot up the whole joint.

Upon arriving there I saw her standing outside with her luggage. There were so many things that I wanted to ask and know but how to bring them up would be a task in itself. What was the update on the baby? If there was a baby, was it mine?

I greeted her with a hug and friendly like kiss on the cheek, to which she did the same thing. As I started driving, she began telling me about her stay at the rehab and how much she felt rejuvenated and cleansed. Apparently, they taught her about God and how asking for forgiveness can heal any broken heart and soul. Something I had no desire to listen to, but I managed to keep from mocking the thought process to avoid a fight and possibly set her back.

The color in her face was now back and she wasn't as frail as she had been while abusing drugs. The glow in her face that originally attracted me to her was now finally back and on top of everything it was a sunny winter day. This January day was a little warm and had plentiful sunshine that matched the relaxation of Patricia. The truth is, I had never seen her so content and healthy. From the time I knew her she was always damaged and ranting about something that didn't go her way. Granted she had every right to complain and desire more than what she had known. Possibly the new Patricia was a person who was going to get the real opportunity to experience all of that.

Something that bothered me till no end was her constant preaching of Jesus Christ and how he is our savior. Patricia was now a loyal follower and had given her heart to Christ and hoped I would do the same thing. To me there wasn't a chance I was going to jump on this Christianity crusade and make believe that bad things won't happen and Jesus will make everything all right. Within the past year I had stopped believing in a God and just accepted what my fate would be when I died. The evidence for a savior and all loving god was nothing more than wishful thinking that rested on a wing and a prayer.

If the belief of God were honestly true then why would there be so much suffering in the world? Why would a loving God have children starve and die everyday? Not to mention the children in the world who are sexually abused by loyal Christian followers and those children who are born with deficiencies that make life almost impossible to live. The negatives of this world by far outweighed the positives. The only logical explanation is that God doesn't really exist.

Like I mentioned before, I didn't want to burst Patricia's bubble so I kept my mouth shut and gave the occasional nod when she was explaining how loving and forgiving he is. We are his children. God made us as a reflection of himself.

Wanting to move the conversation along I asked her if the people she had to live with her were pleasant and if she planned on keeping contact with any of them. She pulled out a notebook where she kept memories and entries of each person she met. Patricia didn't want to forget what had happened and the people she confided in that ultimately helped her.

Mark- Alcoholic who spent his trust fund on old liquor and cheap women but was quite nice and told stupid age-old jokes.

Jane- Abused mother of four who turned to prescription drugs to ease pain, would let me spill my guts about my past to make me feel better.

Jesus Christ Wannabe- talked non-stop about shit no one not even God was interested in hearing. Thought he was a prophet.

Stan #2- Didn't want to admit he had problem snorting coke, but then again who wants to admit it.

Carrie- Girl in her twenties who had sold her body for sex more times than she could count. She got caught cutting herself on more than a couple occasions and is addicted to anything that she could possibly get her hands on.

Old man with hair sticking out of his ears- Probably was an alcoholic back in the sixties when doing dope and anything other available addiction out there was cool. Long hair that was mostly now gray and he had a look that reminded you of a bum or Keith Richards. Sweet though and seemed understanding.

Bobbie- Beautiful girl who had a nice life in the suburbs but threw it away due to her mother's outrageous expectations. Actually was prom queen and voted most likely to succeed. She's a little too broken on the inside but lets her pussy lips hide that.

Drew- a total tool in the making that believes Hes Street smart and could make it in the mafia. Also, he is a total asshole that believes his sarcasm and bad attitude will hide is insecurities and make him seem desirable with women who don't know their vagina lips from the ones on their face, which sometimes have been the same thing for those he has been with.

Nancy- Stubborn underage bitch that was dragged there by her parents to get help. Another case of a kid blaming their parents for all of their failures and missteps. Once you take the time to get to know her you realize she is actually quite pleasant and gentle.

Counselor #1- Dumbass who thinks she can turn peoples lives around, maybe she has a track record that shows she can. Still if you look pass her shortcomings you will find a person just trying to help and we always give points to those people.

Counselor #2- Looking for a paycheck and nothing more. Not too much you can write about an empty person.

Counselor #3- the real counselor who knows his shit and isn't afraid to tell you like it is. Much respect to him.

It was quite funny and sad at the same time to see that these people here are the ones she called her friends but the material written on them seemed to show otherwise. Regardless, it takes all kinds and Patricia met all kinds at the rehab center where she know considered herself a reborn woman. That's nice but she will always be that crazy young bitch to me. And that's what makes me love her I guess; her shortcomings are a turn on. Imagine that.

Patricia and I pulled into the local mall and decided to walk around and take a few looks at some clothing. Not having been out in public in a month she had been starved of the teenage girl lifestyle. It was like letting a kid loose in a candy store or an alcoholic in a liquor store. Spending a ridiculous amount of time in stores such as American Eagle, Hollister, and Aeropostale was not how I envisioned spending my day, but something I was willing to do for the happiness of her. Because no matter how anyone viewed the situation, I had a genuine love and interest in Patricia. Something no one in her life ever truly had. I knew that things were going to have to come to a stop soon and that seeing her was no longer going to be an option. Patricia also took it upon herself to try on every single damn outfit she could. Her sly smile made me suspicious of what she was doing. Every store we left, she had managed to steal something. Whether it was a bracelet or a piece of clothing, she found room in her giant purse for it. Patricia was a regular thief. She would say things like you know we could be the next Bonnie and Clyde. But better looking though, with a smile running across her mouth.

Her mother and father were divorced and she was now going to live with her mother. The closest person to her I guess. Her mother was fine with a "friend" picking her up and bringing her home. If Patricia could stay away from that fucking loser Stan than her chances of staying clean would be greatly increased. She just needed someone by her side to listen and help her. Kind of like something a parent should be. But, Patricia told me that this time was going to be a lot different because her mom was a changed woman and was now interested in being a part of her own daughter's life. I had hoped this to be true because Patricia needed it desperately. After all, she was only a sixteen-year-old girl just trying to find her voice and place in the world.

The truth is, nobody every really finds their voice and place in this world. We all just make good with what we have and tell ourselves that we are fine with everything. After spending all that time in the mall we finally left and headed home. The drive was a tough one because I dreaded with passion at what I had to do. What if she came clean to everyone about our time spent together. Above anything else, I needed to be real with my own reality and emotions. Being real meant not having this tie with a girl who wasn't the legal age and being real meant taking my own responsibilities. Hoping she would finally be done talking about God long enough to let me speak what was on my mind, she just kept rambling on and on.

The genuine love and hope in her eyes was hard to look at because I knew what was to follow. It wasn't until much latter that I realized that Patricia was just a girl and not a woman. Just a teenager trying to make it in today's world that is full of people and opportunity to bring you down to their level. I felt sick to my stomach with guilt.

I was possibly the reason for this whole situation happening and now I was too far deep into my own shit that I didn't know how to get out. What was worse is that I made someone else stuck in my own shit. Patricia was constantly telling me how she was better looking than any other girl there. The counselors were always jealous of my natural beauty she said.

I pulled into her driveway and put the car in park so I could tell her what was needed to be said. She jumped at the opportunity to talk again and this time it was making me telling her the truth even more complicated. Patricia thanked me for being by her side and for always listening to her and being the person she needed me to be. This led to her leaning in for a kiss, but my instincts kicked in and I pulled away before she was able to do so. I looked at her and spoke the words that would change our relationship forever. My thoughts started to become cloudy, my palms were sweaty, and my breaths were getting shorter and harder to fake. Patricia, this is the last time we are going to be able to see each other. A puzzling look came over her face and I went on to say her age got in the way and that constantly going after her and doing what I can to make this work was too much and we both needed to get on with our lives. Ending my break up speech I handed her all the letters she wrote to me while in rehab including the psychotic journal which took me several times to make sense of. She had this stunned look on her face and looked like she was going to lose all control.

Patricia sat in the vehicle and proceeded to cry. There was nothing I wanted to do more than put my arms around and her tell her things were going to be ok. Oh God, I wanted to take back everything that I had done but it was too late for any of that. But I knew that I had to stand firm to make this breakup final. My heart felt like snapping into a million pieces and the tears were starting to form in my eyes. Doing all I could to hold them back I spoke in a low voice, I think you should leave now, I have places and things I need to tend to.

Getting out of the vehicle with tears swimming down her face she looked at me and said well I was going to wait to tell you but as I see this is the last time we will be seeing each other, this news ought to be great for you to hear. I'm not fucking pregnant you asshole. I'm not fucking pregnant. Slamming the door behind her I watched as she ran through her yard and into the house. Leaving her luggage in the yard and the notebooks that she had previously given me.

Watching her leave I couldn't help but to stare. If she looked back just once while going into her house I'd know that she still had feelings for me. Just turn around and look at me. Just one look back and I would know that there was still a place in her heart for me and I just wasn't convenient for her. Sadly enough, she never turned around once.

In that moment, she was to me just a child. A child that I took advantage of like so many other guys have and left when it wasn't no longer convenient for me. If it were up to me I would have stayed with her for as long as she liked, but I knew the truth and what was the right thing to do. Pulling away from her house I just parked my car and sat in it for a few hours. I couldn't believe that the whole mess with Patricia was finally over with. It was in many a way a relief. I no longer was going to be a father and the emotional roller coaster with her was now finally coming to a stop. I could finally get on with my life.

One of the notebooks stayed in my vehicle and as I looked through it I found numerous love letters written to me that she never sent. Patricia put down every thought and feeling she had ever had into that notebook. The one I didn't get the chance to read was now sitting right next to me in my vehicle. The letter that tore me to pieces was harder than hell to read.

Patricia letter #5

For the first time in my life I feel things are starting to look up. I have a boyfriend and my mom seems to want to be a part of my life this time around. I wonder if my dad will have the same realization as she did. Always never feeling like a fit in, I found something at that rehab that I don't think I would have had the chance to find if not for falling flat on my face. Though a few years older than me my new found boyfriend seems genuine enough to take own my child that I'm not sure is his yet and has taken it upon himself to drop me off here and pick me up. I'm looking forward to getting out of here and making this work this time. Maybe there is a God afterwards.

<u>After All I've been through</u>

Teach me how to smile in a world full of pain
Where killers walk the street
And the children are insane
Stones across a dry filled lake
Like glass falling from a mirror

The pieces may fall
But the heart only breaks
How much more can one man take?

How do I say that I love you?
After all I've been through
It's easy to die with the crowd
When there's no one here left allowed
Loving with a dagger in your hand
You're fucking me while you kill your man
The shade of my hearts turned blue
After all I've been through
After all I've been through

Sweetheart you know you can't end it like this
Your presence felt but your heart I miss
I don't know where the hell this is
Cold inside after our last kiss

Leaving Patricia left two songs in my head forever. Cat Stevens "Wild World" always made me think of her. The song had so much feeling and emotion to it that it was like it was written exactly for her. But the song that summed up that day would play in my head for what seemed like eternity. The Manhattans "Kiss and Say Goodbye"

Every time I came home for a weekend or break I would always drive past her house in hopes of seeing her again. She was the love of my life and now she is a past thought. The sad part for me was I never saw her when driving around in her neighborhood.

Kiss and Say Goodbye

This has got to be the saddest day of my life
I called you here today for a bit of bad news

I won't be able to see you anymore
Because of my obligations, and the ties that you have
We've been meeting here everyday
And since this is our last day together
I wanna hold you just one more time
When you turn and walk away, don't look back
I wanna remember you just like this
Let's just kiss and say goodbye

[Song]
I had to meet you here today
There's just so many things to say
Please don't stop me 'til I'm through
This is something I hate to do
We've been meeting here so long
I guess what we done, oh was wrong
Please darlin', don't you cry
Let's just kiss and say goodbye (Goodbye)

Many months have passed us by
(I'm gonna miss you)
I'm gonna miss you, I can't lie
(I'm gonna miss you)
I've got ties, and so do you
I just think this is the thing
To do
It's gonna hurt me, I can't lie
Maybe you'll meet, you'll meet another guy
Understand me, won't you try, try, try, try, try, try, try
Let's just kiss and say goodbye (Goodbye)

(I'm gonna miss you)
I'm gonna miss you, I can't lie
(I'm gonna miss you)
Understand me, won't you try

(I'm gonna miss you)
It's gonna hurt me, I can't lie
(I'm gonna miss you)
Take my handkerchief, wipe your eyes
(I'm gonna miss you)
Maybe you'll find, you'll find another guy
(I'm gonna miss you)
Let's kiss and say goodbye, pretty baby
(I'm gonna miss you)
Please, don't you cry
(I'm gonna miss you)
Understand me, won't you try
(I'm gonna miss you)
Let's just kiss
And say goodbye
<u>Property of The Manhattan's</u>

The feeling of letting someone you love goes is something that is tough to do. I felt like my world had fallen out underneath me. Separating myself from Patricia had nothing to do with me not loving her. In fact, that was the reasoning behind it. Loving her was something I had been doing for a long time and it needed to be put away. If I kept on that same train we would have crashed even harder than we previously had done. Seeing the person you invested so much time and love into walk away feels like a knife through the heart. And no matter how many times you think you have pulled that knife out it still remains there.

Sometimes it is best to leave the knife in your heart for a while. It let's you continue to think straight and come to grips with what you did. Allowing you to realize that what was done was indeed the right thing to do. As soon as you take that knife out of your heart, blood will come pouring out and the feeling of lost will give itself meaning beyond your wildest imagination. Slowly you start to question every decision you ever made and you start to retrace your steps until you find yourself right back where you started and those same mistakes keep happening and you can't even imagine why you continue to do it.

My heart was like a promise made to be broken. It took me sometime to get over Patricia. She was a girl I had no intention on ever loving and all of sudden she came out of nowhere and got me off guard. That's the worse kind of heartbreak. Sometimes you can see a heartbreak coming and it makes the whole process a little easier because you know what to expect and in some way you know that it is going to happen. But when you are unprepared and just cruising along in life and out of nowhere it happens it makes you into a different person. You become a better person than you ever thought you could be.

The voice inside you is happy all the time and your tone is beautiful. You start to treat everyone around you like gold and suddenly you understand his or her problems and want to help out just because you feel so damn good. It is as though life has finally made sense and you're willing to explore any rhyme and reason. The answers you find make you smile and all the pain around you just vaporizes.

Once that love inside of you turns to pain, so does everything else. Now there are no logical answers and everyone is a fucking jerk and life is now a chore and not an opportunity. The color of your heart is no longer red but cooled with a blue that leaves your body frozen to others. Love is just a cruel an unusual punishment instead of a wonderful mystery. So in many ways love is the ultimate killer. It is at the root of everything whether you can admit that or not.

And now I was that person. The person who saw life has a glass half empty. The world was also a lonely place once again. But I couldn't allow that to affect me no more. I had to get back to school and move on with my life. A new leaf was about to turn and I didn't want to miss it, so I took all that pain and stored it away in my mind. My only concentration was my grades.

Well the day came that my winter break would be over with and I had to repack my things to head back to school. The drive up there was refreshing in that it felt like my life was getting a new opportunity. When I arrived it was as though nothing had changed. The people and the way things were when I first moved into that college dorm at the beginning of last semester. As much as I was looking forward to going back I knew that the semester was going to be trial and error one. Many of the teachers in my major department didn't like me because of the trouble that had occurred between me and my previous teacher whom I punched out in a strip club. Again the grade I got was unfair and to add salt on my wound he had told all the other teachers how unreliable I was and how much I loved to start up trouble when something didn't go my way. So right off the bat I knew I had my work cut out for me.

For the longest time I spent days dodging dirty looks and unfair disadvantages. Doing all that I could do to prove myself I turned every assignment early and put my best effort into each word I typed. Taking my entire discontentment in life I wrote papers about how I felt towards everything and just how fucked everything truly was.

My own literary teacher saw my writing as a strong point and said he agreed with much of what I had to say. He even took the time out to point to me that I should have been around in the sixties where I could be surrounded with individuals with like wise minds. But the last thing I wanted was to be surrounded by people similar to me.

Once I was finally done unpacking and getting things settled in, I just lay on my bed and thought about the year I was having. Hoping that whatever damaged that occurred between Mia, Dani, and myself would be forgotten and everyone would just continue to move on. That was nothing but a hope that wouldn't happen.

Mia wasted no time in coming into my room to tease me about our experience just a couple weeks ago. She also went on to tell me that her and Dani were no longer friends and that they weren't rooming together this time around. Mia found it necessary to run Dani into the ground every chance she got. Saying things like did you know that she is just a virgin? I don't think she has ever even let a guy stick his fingers in her prissy little cunt. What a fucking prude and loser, Mia added. Wanting her to go away I just kept nodding and closing my eyes while lying on my bed hoping she would get the hint that I didn't give a rat's furry ass about whatever she had to say.

Girls are never friends for more than a month or two at the same time. Sure, they may become friends again but it won't go without someone talking something nasty about another person. I could never stand mouthy bitches. Girls that do nothing but make fun of people to cover up for their own insecurities. What is the most troubling is that girls will do all that they can to hurt their own friends. They truly don't want that friend of theirs to find a guy to treat them right because that would mean they were now the loser in the friendship or they like being the only girl with a guy that is worth having. The lies they spread about one another is ridiculous as well. Even if the things they are saying are indeed true, no one cares to hear about them. Except, for people with nothing better to do with their lives but prey on the heartaches of others. Which unfortunately our society is covered with them like a bad disease or rash that won't ever go away.

If the things being said about Dani were true, that only means she hasn't faltered under the pressure of everyone around and still has values invested in her mind. I was hoping those things were true because it gave me a respect for her that I previously didn't have. There is nothing attractive about a girl that has been screwed by dozens of men.

Trying to get back to my nap, James had walked in and we proceeded in a conversation. The conversation began with both of us apologizing to one another for what had occurred towards the end of the semester. The truth is, he never intentionally did me wrong, it was something that happened without much thought put behind it. Getting past what had happened was easy and things between us went back to way they use to be.

James and I went to the local bar to grab a few drinks and just reminisce on past good times. When we got there we sat down and the bartender was none other than Dani. She had looked a little different since the last time I seen her a month ago. Her hair was dyed a reddish-brown color, which complimented her eyes quite a bit. Along with her sudden physical change her ass was tighter and her cheekbones seem to have been raised. Indeed she looked different than what I had remembered.

At first we just said hello and went about our stay there with her stopping by only a few times to refill our drinks. Though listening to James talk about the troubles he had encountered on his stay back home, my mind was focused around Dani. I should have been listening to James on the account that he had always listened when I needed someone to talk to. But I couldn't help it; Dani's sudden appearance was mesmerizing. I had thought about everything Mia had told me. Like how she never slept with man or had any real dirty experience. This made her much more desirable to me. James continued on and after a few more drinks we both were wasted and were opened to talking about anything. This led to him noticing my constant attention on Dani, so he gave me the chance to capitalize on it by leaving. I let him know that I would meet him back at the dorm in a little while.

With James gone, I made my way over to Dani's side of the bar and started a conversation. Asking her how her vacation was and if she was looking forward to getting back to class. Her responses were kept to a minimum but she was nice in her tone. I just kept wondering if she knew that I had slept with Mia. Knowing Mia the way I did I had that feeling Dani knew everything that had happened that night. The worse part was that I paid Mia forty dollars. This was no way to attract a girl.

Since I had arrived to college I paid close attention to Dani. Even when I was head over heels about Patricia I always wondered about Dani. I also wondered how much of that night she remembered when she was drunk and if she knew she had spilled her guts out about her problems. Sitting there all alone I started to wonder if I should just go back to the dorms and call it a night. As I began to get up and leave a tip I felt a hand on my shoulder. It was Dani asking me to stay and bullshit with her. Feeling happy now we sat there and I listened inventively to her talking about her vacation. Apparently, she had a pretty good one at that. Explaining how relaxing it was and just the getaway did her wonders. Thinking of ways to connect with her I just agreed with everything she said with a smile.

I had told her that Mia stopped by my room and explained how they weren't rooming together and that their relationship was over. Obviously, I didn't tell her all the gruesome details that Mia had conveyed to me about Dani. Dani just smiled and said that Mia was on one of her rants and that she was just too much to worry about so she asked her to find another place to stay at for school. The calmness in her voice surprised me. It was as though, she already knew what Mia was saying about her and didn't care at all. She just shrugged it off as Mia being loud and immature. There was no doubt she was right and her calmness made Mia look like the psycho bitch she truly was.

This turned me on in a way I have never been excited. Dani was the first girl that I shown interest in that didn't have a mountain full of problems. She wasn't crazy, she wasn't an addict, and she wasn't a slut either. This gave her a lot of brownie points with me. Not that she couldn't have me anytime she wanted anyway.

She was just this wonderful girl that had a vision of how and what she was all about. Again the first time I ever interacted with a girl like this. It was refreshing to say the least. The night was coming to a close and now that Dani was done with her shift I decided to walk her back to campus. For the first time in a long while I had spent time with a female that didn't end up a disaster. There was no sex or perverted goings this time and the only thing between us was a little flirting and a sophisticated conversation.

When we arrived to her building I let her know how much fun I had talking with her and for her letting me unload my problems to her. The problems I told her were made up, there was no way I was going to tell her what had really happened in my life over the past month or so. Instead I created pity problems that only a girl would like to hear.

On my walk back to the dorms a thought crossed my mind about myself that was truer than anything ever said or thought about me. And that was I fall in love with every girl I meet. It's not my fault and not something I can change. The female race has a powerful effect over me. Every girl that I see I fall in love with. Whether it last for a few seconds or a lengthy period the statement in true. I was so focused on not fucking things up with Dani that I knew I couldn't make a move towards her. It would only end like everything else in my life to this point. And that is a complete and utter disaster.

Finally reaching my room, I heard yelling that gave me an unsettling feeling inside. Opening the door I saw Stan just leaning up against my bed arguing with James. All of sudden I had the most fiery rage kick in and I grabbed a hold of Stan and threw his worthless piece of shit ass to the ground. Jumping on top of him I continued a flurry of punches to his face until I felt James throwing me off of him. Lying there with his face covered in blood Stan swayed from side to side in pain. James was panicking like I never seen him panic before, screaming fuck, fuck, fuck. You shouldn't have done that man you shouldn't have done that.

Stan has connections with people that can start trouble with you that you don't want. Trust me. Oh shit man, oh shit. Stan managing to get back on his feet looked over to me and said you better learn to control yourself because next time you won't be so lucky. Saying this with a knife in his hand made him feel like he was strong and independent. Picking up his stuff, Stan finally left. James explained that the argument consisted of Stan asking a favor from him in which he couldn't deliver. James wouldn't tell me what the favor was so I could assume it was something illegal that could get him in a lot of trouble.

Asking me to stop talking to him like he was little kid, I just dropped the whole conversation altogether. Like I mentioned on several rants before, I hated Stan. I hated that motherfucker with a passion. He managed to get an underage girl become a drug addict and lose herself and now he was fucking James life up. He had this way of making people fear and trust him. A strange but lethal combination. I knew as long as he was in the picture that trouble would always follow.

James and I just sat up the rest of that night bullshitting about several different topics. I couldn't get my mind off of Dani. I wanted something positive in my life and she was just the right thing.

This time when James was talking I listened. It became apparent that James was spiraling out of control. He was no longer this guy that everyone wanted to be, that partied with beautiful girls and the only sleeping he did involved a nap after sex. James was stressed out and his financial situation was in the shits. Trying to find money to stay in school was a hard task. He needed money and his family needed money. That was just cold hard facts that no one could deny.

To make up for the lack of money he decided to take on many jobs from Stan to solve that problem. These jobs gave him plenty of money to stay in school and actually start to pay off some of his loans. He could also afford to give his family some much-needed money. But money like this being made when you don't have a legal job or work as a manager only means you are doing something illegal and that was exactly what James was now doing.

He explained nervously that he was selling drugs. Not just simple things like marijuana. But heroin and cocaine. Dangerous things that if fucked up can put you away in the slammer for a long time or if mishandled killed by the others involved. James was now lost in a world he had no business being in. And the person behind all of this was none other than the snake like Stan.

I wanted to kill Stan. I wanted to rip his throat out and watch him bleed to death. To see the life being drained from him would only make me happy. I didn't care about the possibility of going to a non-existent hell. A world without Stan is a better world for all of us.

Lying there that night James began to go deep into detail about his life. Telling me things no one ever knew. As soon as you think nothing can shock or surprise you think again. He never knew his biological parents. The poor kid has been moved around from family to family. Or should I say from so called family to so-called family. Apparently, the reason that he has been moved around so much has nothing to do with his behavior. The reason falls in that he has some medical conditions that people don't want to deal with. He has extreme panic attacks and sometime blacks out and disgustingly bleed from his nose at the same time. Also, he has to take medication all the time to keep from having seizures. I really do feel bad for him. No one asks to be born into this world. No one asks to be different and to be picked on like they are some type of freak without feelings. James says that six months after his birth his parents were killed in a car accident. The way it was explained to him was that a couple of kids were driving drunk and playing chicken with passing vehicles and when they were heading towards his parents, his father swerved to miss them and he hit a tree, killing them on impact. I didn't let him or anyone see it, but I cried when I heard that. He tells it in a very low and desperate voice. I don't believe this kid has ever been truly loved by a hand that has touched him.

James and I have become close friends and that is something that really has helped both of us extremely. It is nice to have someone to tell your troubles to and have them not judge you. We exchange one fucked up story with another. And actually sometimes we laugh about it because it is so typical. We are both truly the outsiders on this campus.

Sometimes I wonder about James. He is the loneliest individual I have ever seen. Just to sit in ones own lonely room and stare at a wall can't be healthy. He and I are so similar. We come from different places and people. We have different stories but by the end of the day we want the same things out of life. We feel the same about life. I do worry about him. He has so much anger and hurt inside of him that it is just a matter of time until something else happens.

Where is God? Where is he when things get so rough that you can't even stand on your own two feet? Does he think of us as rejects and losers as society does? Does anyone know God? What is religion? Maybe pain is like a test to reach heaven.

Because of Stan, James was now living a life of decadence. Who is going to love me? I ask this question so much but I never know the answer. Or the answer that I want anyhow. When I walk into a store people look around at me as though I'm a thug. Like I am going to steal something. I'm just a person. Why can't they just let me be? I just want to be loved.

Dear lord, when will this hell stop for me? Have you ever just wanted to scream? Have you ever thought that you couldn't take any more pain and if you did you just might die from it? I do. See my lonely life unfold. The heartache of everything is just insane. It is just way too much for anyone to handle.

Like I mentioned before, James was no longer the person everyone knew and loved. The changes were rapid and severe. I wondered about him on a day-to-day basis. Everything that had occurred in his life was now finally catching up to him and he was running out of ways of coping with it. On top of it all, he now was indulging himself in selling drugs. Another way to dig him deeper in a hole that has no way has climbing out of.

<u>CLOSING DOORS</u>

Can we take a stroll down memory lane?
Hand in hand and feel the same
In your time am I insane
While I hold you in vain
Let's love today and drown in tomorrow
While I fill a sea deep with sorrow
And drink its sin with pain again

They love you for the things you can buy
They hate you for what you feel inside
They let you bleed till their pain dies
But in the end son you can only serve yourself
And to this and to no one else

127

Let me tell you about the faces of evil
That is knocking at your door

A smiling face turns into a stalker
A sweet hello can become darker
Than the blood from Satan's heart
Never let the stranger of insanity
Walk you through the window of opportunity
Cause hope and faith shut like a door
And in hell dreams are no more

I'll paint the days
While you're bleeding the years
You change your ways
They'll show you new fears
They hurt you with what they say
But don't let them see you cry your tears
Cause the end will appear much closer and clear

Cause you're close to realizing
The meaning of life
When you gotta take it for what its worth
Or you'll end up another lost soul on this earth
Cause nothing ventured my son
Is nothing gained?
Spend your life working for a cause you can't define
All they want is your work and all your time
They take away your last breath and thought
Without a care

Jesus arms won't close around me
I can't stop myself from falling
Like the morning sun in the summer raining
I feel this life is soon ending

Church doors close in my eyes
That's not how I feel
That's not who I am
I don't understand

Chapter 8
A Little Below The Angels

Beauty on the lips of a lie
It makes you want to live
Her kiss makes you want to die
Madness on the tip of your tongue
Razor blade sharp its faith is done
Memories are just infestations of the mind
You search for answers yet the key you never find
The moon settles as the morning sun shines
Where the dawn breaks with nighttime's crimes
Angels make demons of us all
Like spring turns to summer and dies in the fall
Drowning endlessly in time
Sometimes is our wake up call
To a life near perfect
To a death never lived at all

When I was just a little kid my father took me by the hand and walked me along the fence by our house and had a talk with me. He said there are things in life that a man must understand. And there are things in which will confuse you for a lifetime. The things that a man must know are acquired in time and with years that make up wisdom. My father was a man of few words and when he spoke, people in the house listened. I was so confused with our talk that it left me wanting more and more information on what he was talking about. He went on to explain such things to me though. Wisdom my son is not gained through books or with God given talent. Wisdom is life itself. Wisdom is what's happening to you while you are living and its failing and succeeding and knowing when you've done what you could and when to get out.

His father used to tell him that a wise man learns from his mistakes but a wiser man learns from others. After this, I decided to go for a walk myself. I walked for miles out in the countryside. I walked till I just couldn't walk anymore. In doing so, I had a lot of time to think. Time left alone I would find out later can turn into time that should always be left alone. I started to wonder deeply about the meaning of life. Why are we here? What is my purpose in this world? Is it a sin to question God and the afterlife? I started to feel so alone in the world and nobody had the answer to any of these questions. Sure, there are religious men out there and those that do nothing but bullshit themselves just to sleep better at nights. But really, what is life?

I really didn't understand the significance of that talk and walk with my father. Early on in life I guess that I learned just how precious life is. I learned not to take things for granted and with a drop of a hat the life you are living can turn around into something that is merely a memory. The older I got the harder my feelings became and the more wisdom I gathered the keener my eyes became. People from all walks of life may seem very different to you and they may seem to have nothing in common. Especially in religion, fashion, and pop culture but inside of them lies something that you can relate with more than anything in the world. I continued along with my walk with this sticking in my brain. When I was on my walk I found a rock and for some reason, I kept it. I just starred at this plain old rock for hours. I never really understood the significance behind it. I was just fascinated with the simplicity of this object. The shape and curves and natural form of time that it has gained. When I woke up I realized this was just another dream. Why did all of my dreams bring me back to my childhood?

It's 3:23 in the morning and I'm lying in my bed staring at the ceiling. Everyone is sleeping and the entire house is silent. My thoughts are running rampant and I just can't seem to keep my eyes closed long enough to fall asleep.

Finally tired of lying there I decide to get up and go outside and just breathe in the summertime air. While I'm out there I find myself getting into my car and pulling out of the driveway. Cruising down the road I am going just under the speed limit and I'm taking in everything around me. The trees, houses, lawns, and signs that are surrounding me. I find that the faster I go the less I see and remember the scenery. With my foot on the pedal I continue to go faster and faster and soon I look at the speed dominator and I'm flying going at ninety-five miles per hour and even one hundred at times.

Soon everything around me is just a blur and my thoughts are racing at a million miles per hour and nothing is sinking in anymore. My body feels paralyzed except for my feet. My mind is lost and disarray and confusion and nothing seem to make sense. For some reason, I'm afraid to turn around in the vehicle for fear that someone or something is behind me getting ready to attack. It's as though I know my death is coming, but I rather have it sneak up on me rather than see it coming and feel all the effects from it.

In a way, all of this is just like life. The faster we go the faster we get to our death. We don't allow ourselves to appreciate all the beautiful things that surround us everyday. We are taking it all for granted and we keep going faster and faster and soon we are at our deaths and we are just left questioning everything we have ever been taught. Wondering where did the time go? How did all of this come to be? Even, when we see disasters before us we decide to put on blinders in hope that the situation will just disappear and dissolve itself. Our mind starts playing nasty tricks on us and convincing us the less we feel the less we will be harmed.

But, in hindsight is we will end up feeling a lot more and the feelings won't be kind.

But just like when I was in the vehicle, the slower I went the more I got to take in. The chance to experience everything increases greatly and starts to develop our minds and thoughts into something we can understand and take comfort in. All of sudden our blood pressure decreases and slowly but steadily our body relaxes and we are at one with ourselves. The realization that life is short starts to take on a whole new meaning and it's a positive one because we are realizing it before we are too old to do anything about it. For some reason, life suddenly has a purpose and we aren't screaming all the time and our problems become simple solutions. But, be careful not to start living in fantasy because that's just as dangerous.

The time I spent in the vehicle slowly turns minutes into hours and the sun is just about to rise. Still going at a speed of one hundred miles per hour I see a figure in the rising fog but I'm not sure if it's a person standing there or an animal. As I'm slamming on the breaks the car starts to twist and turn out of control. Too late to stop, I realize the figure in the fog is a man and in a blink of an eye I crash right into him. Right as I begin to hit the windshield I wake up.

This time upon waking up I am greeted with a telephone call. The words I'll never forget being spoken over the phone. James is dead. I couldn't believe it, the blood in my face felt like it completely flushed out. My heart as though it had fallen out of my chest. My body is numb in a way I never imagined. The first logical thought in my mind is if I were there none of this would have happened. I let him down. I let him down.

6:47a.m. Saturday January 14th James was found dead. The police cars were surrounding the dorm and his foster parents just had this blank stare on their face like they didn't know just what to do. I ran through the yellow caution tape and pushed through the cops and ran into our room. There he was with a white sheet pulled over top of him. James had committed suicide. I didn't believe what my eyes were seeing. Another bombshell had just exploded. Why did he do this to himself? Actually I knew why he did this to himself. James was a lonely kid who never felt real love. He never knew the good life had in store and he never was close to anyone but me. He never told me he was going to do it and I lost a brother. He wasn't blood but he was as close as blood got. He left a not by himself that read

> Loneliness in my heart and in my dreams
> Loneliness is more pain than it seems
> Eats you alive and leaves nothing
> Where you had hope of something

Shadows of Pain

Let's hide away
Another day
For tomorrow's pain
Is just another day away
And let our emotions swim in the river
For they're more free
Than our minds can say
Without troubles and delay

Shadows of pain
Are following me, everywhere I stand
They know me and the things I see
My thoughts our my yesterdays
They see me running away
If you touch then you can feel
These wounds are far too real
For one man to hide and another to steal
The times are turning like these wheels

Morning sun rising in my window

Glimpse of heaven in my tomorrow

Time spent sometimes is time borrowed
Love like a bird in the sky
Temporary are our goodbyes
When the eye rains with a cry
There becomes an answer to our why
Don't you feel sorry for me

Cause I'm my own worst enemy

I didn't cry when he killed himself. It just felt like another brick in the wall. What do you really say when something like this happens to someone you know. Sorry? What ashame? James was always popular in school and he had two things that he loved. They were drawing and football. He had all the skills to succeed in sports. How could he? He never had a father or role model around to show him how to do anything. Everything he knew was a result of busting his ass just to make it. He got cut from the football team during tryouts and he never got the mental help he deserved. He was treated like a number instead of a person. Never given the time or day in anyone's life. People always wonder how something like this happens. You don't have to look any further than how you treat someone. A simple hello or how are you can make the biggest difference in someone who has so little in the lives. People just want to be accepted. They just want to feel like they are part of the crowd and piece of the puzzle. Instead they are the person that doesn't quite fit in the puzzle. You know the piece that is just too bent or twisted to fit in where it is suppose to go. I thought I knew James. And I did somewhat but you are only going to get to know something from someone unless you take the time to get to know the whole part instead of certain pieces. I never forgot how I reacted to James telling me about Stan and his drug associates. That feeling would stick with me until the day I die. I don't know how some people wake up in the morning and live with them.

James was just a kid stuck in a man's body that never got the real chance to grow. Nothing like anyone else on that campus made him stand out and be popular and envied. With already enough load from his past it didn't help that James dived head first into drugs. The cops raided the room and found cocaine spreaded out everywhere. He kept it hidden from me when I would go home and then spread it all out when he knew he would be the only one in the room for a certain time.

The monkey that wouldn't get off of his back was a prescription drug that was given to him by doctors that wanted to help with his latest football injury. Like any person who allows them to get run by a life full of drug dependence, James paid the ultimate price. One of the worse parts in all of this was I didn't know anything about it. He kept it hidden from me and I had no chance to try to save him like I did for Patricia.

I never would have figured James was too the point where he felt death was his only option. But, I wasn't there. I wasn't there. I let him down. I let him down.

The anger raged inside of me like a wildfire that couldn't be stopped. I never felt such a mixture of feelings that consisted of lost, loneliness, and rage. And the worst part of this was there was nothing I could do about it. There wasn't one mother-fucking thing I could do about this. I thought about all the parties and good times we will never have a chance to have. I wouldn't get the chance to have that in my life. Not now. Not ever.

Right now though, that doesn't matter. Nothing is mattering at the moment other than my grief. It's a sunny

Sunday and I'm pulling myself together to attend my best friend's funeral. The thought of James being dead was just beginning to hit the surface of my heart and leave an imprint. He was essentially the only true friend I have ever had. James knew how to live his life and he knew that time was always precious. Still, it didn't stop him from killing himself. At the height of his youth he kills himself. What a waste of genuine talent and a genuine person.

How do we as humans deal with situations that we never quite prepare ourselves for? Making our minds believe something so whole-heartedly that we can't imagine anything other than that being true often proves harmful. Suicide is something that leaves us asking questions until the day you are dead. The thought of someone you love taking his or her life makes you take on a different approach to your own life. Its something you never imagine happening until it's too late. The signs, which everyone finds so obvious usually, are anything but. We spend so much time and energy learning how not to feel that when the time comes that we have to deal with our emotions we have no clue how to anymore. Our sleepless self help society has drained us of every single coping mechanism out there and has replaced it with books and pills that are written by people who don't have a clue on how to make their own lives right let alone counsel others on their emotions and thoughts on life.

We wake up everyday and put on every kind of mask we can find to hide ourselves away from the world. Not realizing at the time we are just cruising on by in life and not fully understanding exactly who we are. People spend their whole lives trying to figure out who they are and they try on different faces in the process. This though is healthy. You got to experiment and do tests run with a few different perspectives to find out which one fits you the best. But the trouble in that lies with taking the perspective on yourself that everyone takes on you and decides it fits you best. Instead of finding the one that makes you truly you.

Do your demons
Do they ever let you go
when you've tried?
Do they hide?
Deep inside
is it someone that you know
you're a picture
Just an image caught in time
we're a lie
You and I
We're words without a rhyme
-Ronnie James Dio-

     I didn't want to be seen around anyone. I just wanted to be left alone. No one understood and knew what was happening and the things that were running through my head at a hundred miles per hour. How could they? They didn't lose their best friend. I was surrounded with a bunch of fake people with fake sympathy. I just didn't need the world and its ways at this time.

     Before they buried James I got to have an hour with him alone. I sat there next to the casket and just poured my heart out. How can such a terrible thing happen? I was cheated out of a friend. I was cheated out of a friendship of pleasant memories. I held his hand before they came in and took him away. My voice was rough and very teary. I spoke my last words to him.

James:
I don't know how to say goodbye
I don't know how to let it show
I bet somewhere in heaven
Your are smiling and will let me know
That you are fine

And in life everything must go
Every season and year has its end
Yours too soon
I just wanted to say
I lost my best friend.

Well, I guess that is it. I guess that is it. Goodbye. I will see you again one day. We will catch up on all of those talks that we will never have. We will catch up on those memories that were swept away. We will catch up on arguing and say all the things that we forgot to say. I love you.

I decided that the only place of peace for me was down at that old dirt road where I would spend taking walks and talks with my father. The difference this time was not only was it dark but I was alone. And in my mind I could only help to think that alone is how the rest of my life would be. I sat at that rock like a have a million times before and just threw pebbles into that old lake and just blanked out. I didn't think about anything and I didn't feel anything. I just was numb and that was the first thing I could call mine and only mine my whole life it seemed. It was like nothing existed and nothing mattered. It was just this surreal dream and I was the only thing that existed. How is that for different? After while I thought about James and the type of man he was. I thought about the things in life he liked and the things he hated. I thought about how his days were and what could have been going through his mind when he knew he was about to die.

The next morning I woke up in bed. The strange thing is I don't remember just exactly how I got there. That place along the countryside was the last place I remember being just before I fell asleep. But oh well I just probably was having that numb feeling where I don't remember things.

If Darkness were an hour

139

I'd be the day
If the grapes in life weren't sour
We'd express what we say
If God's grace grew the flowers
I know how you'd feel
In each and every way

I wake up and I get out of bed and everything is still the same. There is no change in the wind of depression. There are no Mayflowers or summer sunshine beaming off of my face. Just the debris of what is formerly known. Am I the only person who wanders in the walk of life not knowing where and who they are? The more we search sometimes the less we find. Perhaps, it is the moments in life when nothing is expected or hoped for when freedom arises. I think that the most complex things in life can be broken down into small explanations. Why do we complicate what is so simple? The essence of life is not the longevity but the moments that you feel alive. Awake yourself from this everyday misery and regret. My child things are simple. Take the wind and the rain for examples. These are God's elements to show he is there. They might not be pleasant but life isn't always pleasant.

Tomorrow was here
But had to go
Where it went
No one really knows
Yesterday came
And the leaves began to change
But for a short time
Was it near and alive?
Or was it like the people in your life
That was here but had to die

Emotions take on a life of their own

Some are awaken and some are alone
They sleep and they breathe by your grace
Like the summer wind kissing your face
And life is but a bittersweet day
That shows hope and a better way
For the lives of so many
Who had so much to say

I started to keep a journal of everything I felt when
he died. The school psychiatrist advised this to me. Maybe it
will help, maybe not. But it did capture what I was feeling.

Have you ever been alone? You know what I mean,
right? Have you ever sat in a bed and looked at the ceiling
and just drifted off into pure thought? I think what keeps
people going in life are not the rewards of living but the fear
of death. The fear of being alone. The fear of waking up and
finding yourself in a mentally solitary confinement.

Many of times we never imagine what we find the
unthinkable. Because where would we be afterwards? Where
would our minds take us if we let them run free and do as
they please? Would we commit the unthinkable crimes of our
youth? Or would we be disappointed to find out that some
of our loved ones are emptier inside than a corpse rotting on
the side of a highway? I'd like to think there are compassion,
love, and understanding in every living thing on this earth.
But for that misleading hope has led to many a men untimely
deaths and mourning.

Maybe if people every now and then could look into
another's soul things would be much clearer. If someone
would look into your soul what would they see or find?
Everyone can look into another person's soul. The eyes are
the gateway to the soul. They are the very essence to decision
making. You can even look through a blind man's soul by
looking into his eyes. His or her eyes can see. Just not in the
way you have been taught. Not in the way we perceive the

world and its functions.

I guess to everyone my life has completely changed. It's sad it took a funeral to bring that out in me. I'm so tired of everyone trying to figure me out like I'm some kind of puzzle or something. I'm just hurting inside and there's nothing I can do to make this hurt go away. Is there anything that will take this surreal pain going away? Why do people have to scrutinize everything I say or do? Just leave me alone. Just leave me alone.

The school seems to be in a time of mourning. The girls he spent nights with and the friends he made all were affected by his leaving us. Everyone looked at me knowing the pact that James and I had with one another. People all around were lost, at a lost of self it seemed. Tomorrow I have to give a speech in front of the college. They thought that it would be good to have someone that has been affected through this incident to give an inspiring speech. That is the last thing they are going to get from me. I plan on giving a speech that will bother many. When it came time to give the speech I felt frozen. I felt numb once more.

I walked up to the podium were it was flooded with questions ranging anywhere from my thoughts on life to what I think about rough times and to the current situations in the third world countries. Standing there with a deep and concentrated look on my face, I said nothing as I stood there. All of sudden I finally spoke calling everyone slaves and that people need to take a better look at themselves and what is wrong instead of asking me questions no one has an answer to. We follow organizations and religious groups because it gives us an identity and sense of self, we feel as though we finally discovered where we belong and what we should be following in this world where materialism is the only thing left and less and less people are living and dying without love. Love is truly the only thing that has survived the test of time. All fashion trends and self-satisfying worldly possessions have all came and gone with the wind. I guess my words shocked and stunned the crowd. They were felt and as though a bomb was just dropped upon the nation. There my speech touched people and confused the feeble minded. I spoke of his after life beliefs. In a way I knew best.

I think we all believe in something that we think will save us in the end. Something in our minds that we think sets us apart from anything and everything. It is funny and strange to me that we treat people like they are nothing and we commit more sins than a demon in hell on a regular basis but we still continue to think that we are above and beyond everyone else. That our needs in some way, shape, and form are above others and that God rather help us and knows us to be good but knows others little as to say they are hell ridden. That is the nice way. Huh?

I kept writing down all the things that I felt were responsible for his death. Things that I thought were behind people taking their own life. Life was behind everything that had occurred. Sort of ironic?

Dear Diary, Mankind's current disrespect and lack of courtesy towards civilization have led us to years of decapitation and self-suffering. We all need to learn to accept individuals as they are and not as whom we want or expect them to be. Put aside everyone's personal beliefs of the after life because it doesn't matter. What matters is here and now and the current state of things to come. Look as the man next to you as your brother instead of your enemy. Open you door and windows of perception. Let the birds sing, let the children cry and let the man weep for himself. We don't need all of this suffering and self-inflicting pain. Unite as one and lets save the earth. Because in the end you need everyone and anyone if you want to survive. The only person that's paranoid is you. Because deep down were not after the other guy, were after ourselves. We take unnecessary precautions to watch our own backs. We need to recognize the other as our savior and come together as one.

All of our men and woman of little knowledge and faith come to your senses. The dirt is brown and heavy like our hearts that are bleeding through; we tend to put on a mask that makes us appear dark and cold. Let's drop the chains that hold us back from redemption. We all need a guiding light. When you look into the mirror, what do you see? Do you see a man, a myth, or a just mire image of what you once were or hoped to be? Only the day of true peace can come when our nations and its people let down their guard to lend a helping hand of a man that it drowning in his own pool of tears. Pain isn't always visible. Sometimes the worse form of pain known to man isn't visible in the eyes of the richest at mind. It sleeps in your heart and eats away at your righteous behavior. It can take you like a hurricane in the night. Why must make ourselves suffer? No matter what religion, race, color, or background in the end we all want the same. We want our children and loved ones to be happy. We want to sleep and know that our hard work will show its true labors in the morning. We want to go for a walk and know that all is calm and gentle in the mind of the stranger that passes you. We all just want to be FREE!!!!

I felt the need to reach after I finished my thought of peace. If there is going to be a tomorrow for our society, there needs to be children who are loved, learning, and progressing and with the world in the state it is in we need to reach out and give the future of tomorrow a helping hand. We don't know what tomorrow may bring us. Sometimes to make a difference you need to be the difference. There's always going to be people out there that need a helping hand a set of ears to listen to them. I'm trying to reduce that number and bring peace amongst the people. No child will be turned away based on its culture, race, or religion. I believe of everyone would take a minute or two from their so called busy lives and own personal problems to reach out an help someone who was once in their own shoes the world may be able to gain an ounce of respect for itself.

Success is nice but what is keeping a smile on society's face is waking up every morning and seeing what is and what will never be. There is nothing on this earth more sacred than family. It helps shape your personality, views on the world, and your own personal values. Never underestimate the power of love and its capabilities. Turning on the television and seeing some guy yelling Give Peace A Chance and the foundation people claim to be apart of succeed is pure brilliance. I want to bring the people together and I feel the more we do the more better the daily life will be. I will continue to do what I love. The world needs guidance and understanding and that's what I'm hoping to accomplish. The success of a shot in the heart is sick yet it is a heart warming feeling also. I spent a lot of time working on the world's project and I put my heart and soul into it and the fruits of my labor are definitely showing. Who receiving the Noble Peace Prize is really capable of changing our atmosphere? I want to take the time to thank the people who don't exist fans, family, and our personal drive. I view myself as a man trying to make a difference. We all can do it and we all can put forth the effort.

How much blindness can the world fathom? All I did was lay truth down on this notebook and show the world what really happens behind closed doors. This was meant to offend those of blind faith. Open your eyes and see what has occurred in your everyday life. I have never been about pleasing people who are happy with the current destruction of today's world. I'm all about change for the good. Be the difference.

What's lying around you and what's eating at me are two opposite things in this nature of our world. We are just striving and living for the cause. But do we know just what that cause is or is it just pure fun and fantasy? Do you have a deeper sense of what is real and fabrication of the mind? Well, do you? You never know when the end is near or when a beginning is about to show up right on your front door step little miss sunshine. Shot in the heart can hit you like a ton of fucking bricks. We all should as you say. Right? Right? Right? Right?

John Lennon came on the radio today while I was in room just staring off into nowhere land. The song that was playing was Instant Karma. Those lyrics are so mesmerizing that they kept with me for some time. Not only were they well written but they made sense.

Instant Karma

Instant Karma's gonna get you,
Gonna knock you right on the head,
You better get yourself together,
Pretty soon you're gonna be dead,
What in the world you thinking of,
Laughing in the face of love,
What on earth you tryin' to do,
It's up to you, yeah you.

Instant Karma's gonna get you,
Gonna look you right in the face,
Better get yourself together darlin',
Join the human race,
How in the world you gonna see,
Laughin' at fools like me,
Who on earth d'you think you are,
A super star,
Well, right you are.

Well we all shine on,

like the moon and the stars and the sun,
well we all shine on,
and Ev'ryone comes on.

Instant Karma's gonna get you,
Gonna knock you off your feet,
Better recognize your brothers,
Ev'ryone you meet,
Why in the world are we here,
Surely not to live in pain and fear,
Why on earth are you there,
When you're ev'rywhere,
Come and get your share.

Well we all shine on,
Like the moon and the stars and the sun,
Yeah we all shine on,
Come on and on and on on on,
Yeah yeah, alright, uh huh, ah-.

Well we all shine on,
Like the moon and the stars and the sun,
Yeah we all shine on,
On and on and on on and on.

Well we all shine on,
Like the moon and the stars and the sun.
Well we all shine on,
Like the moon and the stars and the sun.
Well we all shine on,
Like the moon and the stars and the sun.
Yeah we all shine on,
Like the moon and the stars and the sun

     I finished up another diary that would make a true
mark on everything. This diary gave a very innocent and

easy to fall in love feel. It's such a story of an old man that expresses himself in everyway. It was great writing it. It was until I realized that the old man I was writing about is I. I felt pretty confident and nice about this though. I think it brings back that element of innocence before we had the sexuality that is present in our today. Great people express themselves through love but these are the same people that rally against and condemn when someone brings it out in the open and confronts them with it. Let's learn to love and not to hate our neighbor.

If it has to be then we are all just lost souls roaming around in total darkness looking for the road to recovery. If every love that was lost was a death in our hearts then I guess we are just zombies looking for a reason, rhyme, or cause. What is the human heart? Why does it keep us alive? And why do we spend so much time protecting it all the while we abuse it? Is it our nature as human beings to kill and torture us? We strive for good in ourselves yet we look for the worst in others. Maybe we are not the good holy ones God is looking to save and heal. Maybe we are the roadblock that keeps peace from entering into the world and solving its most hated crimes. We just never know how we feel or what we will do in times or desperation and need. It is confusing yet it is beautiful.

Beautiful for the watcher and confusing for the participant. It seems as though we are actors and actresses in a play that doesn't have a necessary script. We are players in the game of life and the penetrated determines the end. Yea, that seems logical and fair. I think the best way out is not to take a deeper look into our eyes. Because that is where the soul is. The soul is our eyes. Our eyes tell everything about us. The let out how we feel and how far we are willing to go to get freedom and love. The soul is just right behind the eyes. The eyes are the front door way to the soul. This friend is a fact not a myth or idea but cold hard fact. How does it all make you feel? How does it all fit in your head? Love is passion and passion is love. Death is birth and yet birth guarantees death. So which is sadder birth or death? Don't let either one determine your mind or your destiny. Because destiny is a road to forgetfulness which leads to the end of time. Destiny is our way of explaining the unknown and fucking the lover of evil. Am I right? Am I wrong?"

God grant me the serenity
to accept the things I cannot change;
courage to change the things I can;
and wisdom to know the difference.

Living one day at a time;
Enjoying one moment at a time;
Accepting hardships as the pathway to peace;
Taking, as He did, this sinful world
as it is, not as I would have it;
Trusting that He will make all things right
if I surrender to His Will;
That I may be reasonably happy in this life
and supremely happy with Him
Forever in the next.
Amen.

Trust in the LORD with all your heart
and lean not on your own understanding;
in all your ways acknowledge him,
and he will direct your paths.

Proverbs 3, 5-6

Angel Tears

Mindless souls across your path
Bloodstain hearts draw a blood stained bath
Once was first now is last
Aligned with judgment under Gods wrath
Ghosts crowd the streets with no name
And their thoughts cry out in shame
With rage from hell in dying fame
All the reasons and rhymes just the same
Your body sleeps but your mind plays the game
Of holocaust survival and paralyzed souls lame

Come with me to the skies of blue
Where heaven rains all is true
And the water drips in ways of new
This is old and gold through and through

Angel Tears
Swimming down your face
Angel Tears
A timeless endless race
Angel Tears
Sleep with comfort in place
Angel Tears
Never say goodbye
Don't you worry or cry
Angel Tears
Soar and fly

Walking through the shadows of death
I reach out see and feel your breath
You speak silence but abhor truth

To the end of this journey
Come with me to the skies of blue
Where heaven rains all is true
And the water drips in ways of new
This is old and gold through and through

Angel Tears
Swimming down your face
Angel Tears
A timeless endless race
Angel Tears
Sleep with comfort in place
Angel Tears

Soar and fly

Look at all of Gods faithful children dying
Dry the tears of the broken hearted mother crying
Lost souls reaching for another day
God only knows there's a better way
Does your end justify your means?
After all the satanic blood spilling you seen
Your death rolling tanks, planes, and suicide missions
Shake a hand of a smile seducing politician
Spread your idea of a loving democracy
While you fill my head with your hypocrisy

Dripping away
Dripping away
Blood on the hands of fate
Blood is the color of hate
Flying high
And soaring low
Flying high
And soaring low

151

A kiss is just a kiss without rape
And a touch is just a touch without feel
And what is certain isn't real

Are we reliving past memories
Newspapers read same ol story
When you find peace give me the key
To escape the blind and set the damned free
Listen to me it's your story to tell
There was seven long years spent in hell
When the devils grasp is something lonely and wicked
So many of life's faithless men souls have died naked
Moments of insanity that satin fed
His whisper of words like a shot to your head
That drops endless beliefs dead
Losing my heart while I cried my soul to sleep
When I hit too hard cause I fell to deep
Like a secret in the night that only one can keep
Days lost in a corpse nights spent to weep

I never wondered how old I'd be when I died,
I always wondered when I'd stop living.
She had long black hair
Hazel in her eyes
A deep blue stare
Gazed with lies

A heart of gold
Broke with love
With a smile grown cold
She was the girl I dreamed of

We use to kiss
So tender and softly
These days I just reminisce

Of holding her tightly

Now she's gone
And I miss her greatly
If you that's wrong
You've never loved deeply

Chapter 9
Goddess in the Doorway

For the first time since James death I decided to walk back into the room. But I had no intention on staying there the least bit. Grabbing my belongings, I knew in the back of my mind that his would be the last time I ever step foot in this room. It was official, I was done with college. The experience was much different than I had ever expected. No one would have imagined his or her experience to be anything like this. I guess I had no choice but to drop out because I never returned for the remainder of the spring semester. During finals week was when I decided to move out for good.

Also, my head was getting a little bit clearer and functioning on a day-to-day basis. With my possessions and thoughts collected I headed out the door and on my out Dani stood there right in front of me. It had been quite awhile since I last talked to her. Since James passing I stopped talking to almost everyone. She asked if I was ever going to come back. Looking sadly at her I said no and my stay there would be permanently over with. Her face suddenly turned very upset as she gave me a hug and places a piece of paper with her phone number on it in my hand. Knowing well that I was going to give her a call, I finally spoke telling her that when I had the time that I would give her a call.

Dani walked with me to my car and during the walk there she expressed how sorry she felt that James was gone and how much she knew we meant to each other. Not wanting to burst out in a cry I just nodded my head in agreement. When we reached my car we both just looked at each other feeling uncomfortable. Dani and I weren't a couple and we never had sex with one another. Plus, we never spent any time with one another except for the drunken walk and the one we took in the beginning of this semester. But something felt different with her than any other time. It was as though we had this bond between the two of us. Maybe inside of each of us we wanted to be together but didn't know how to. The feeling though was warm.

Looking at the realness in her face I just wanted to grab her and hold her. I just wanted to tell her that she could make my life so much easier and that this isn't the way things had to be. Like I have so many times before, I just swallowed whatever emotions I had and kept them locked inside for latter pain and torment.

Closing my trunk we finally said our goodbyes and I took off for the last time. Driving away I just thought how fast time goes when you're not paying attention. The time that had elapsed between the beginnings of the fall semester and now seemed like a long month instead of nine. What was more troubling to me was how much different your life can be in a blink of an eye. Everything about me had changed and it changed rapidly. No longer was I the person I was when I moved into that college dorm. In that time including the summer before college I found myself in love with an underage drug addicted stripper, having random kinky sex, and losing my best friend. That's not your typical pattern in life. Maybe variations of those things are in chronological order but not the specifics.

Time had just sneaked up on me and everyone else I knew for that matter. How I managed to hide this from my parents was incredible though. Involving people in my problems is not how I like to handle things. Too many people I know have to deal with so many others problems that they never find time to heal themselves. This is why I didn't want to add onto my parents my daily struggles.

People have enough to worry about. Besides, if they knew what I had gotten myself into they both might have been in an early grave. One person I loved dying was enough for me anyway.

As I continued to drive, I put my Tom Petty and the Heartbreakers greatest hits into my car stereo. That made the drive more pleasant and it helped put my mind to ease just the same. When the song Mary Jane's Last Dance came on it made me laugh. During the first semester my class had to get into groups and make a play out of a song. My group chose this classic and the play was shameful. They missed the whole point of the song and the realness in his lyrics. I'm not talking about smoking marijuana either. That's not what I was getting at. That led me to fully realizing that I wouldn't be back at that place no longer. No longer would I call that college home. No, instead it would be the place where I lost my best friend and everything that I ever believed in.

When I got back into my hometown I decided to go for a run. Hoping this would also help my troubling mind and that the fresh air would do me good. As I was jogging, I ran passed Patricia's house. This believe it or not wasn't intentional the least bit. While I was running I didn't pay attention to what neighborhood I'd find myself in. I guess instinct is never far from the heart.

Looking as I passed by I saw her in her backyard with a baby in her arms. This made me run even faster than before. Was the baby hers? Did she lie about being pregnant? More of a question was is the baby mine? For some reason I didn't stop. If the baby were mine she would have told me. Even after our last meeting, her mother would have demanded her to tell the father's name. Child support is something every single mother loves. And Patricia was no different in that department. Or was she?

The baby could have possibly been someone else's. A friend, a relative, or she could have just been baby-sitting.

Not knowing for sure was how I left it. I wasn't going to waste anymore time on her and the what it's that came along with everything she ever did or said. So I continued to move along without looking back on it.

Wishing that I could for once in my life stick to my word, I gave Patricia a call and asked how she was doing. Her words were slow and a little lonesome, but she told me that she was doing good and managed to not have relapsed yet. Hoping if I gave a quick chuckle it would ease the conversation along and that's exactly what I did. Patricia had asked me how I was doing with everything because she had heard about James death and wanted to call me but didn't want to stir up any old feelings. Taking a deep breath I explained that it was pretty hard at first but I had managed to move on. Knowing damn well inside that I was just hiding away everything that I actually felt I told her that sometimes life just goes that way.

No one understood the way that I truly felt about her. Patricia was my drug in every sense you could think of, I knew that being with her was death to my mind but an instant relief for the moment and I just wanted someone there. I got tired of always being lonely and I just needed someone there to spend some time with. With that note, I told her that I just dropped out of school and wanted to take a trip down south to see a few baseball spring training games and just unload some of this baggage. She quickly responded asking if I had anyone to go along with. That's when I jumped in and told her that it was the reason I was calling because I needed an extra person to make the trip just a little bit more memorable.

Once again pulling into her driveway, Patricia came running out all smiles and jumped into my pre-owned 1998 ford probe. We both didn't know what to expect from one another as I pulled out and headed down to Florida for the week. The drive seemed to never end as Patricia slept for most of the way there. Whenever she woke up, she would quickly turn the radio station I was listening to and put something that I considered god awful on. That was a trait in Leah that I found very attractive, but this Patricia and she never was Leah.

As we arrived to Florida, Patricia insisted on me pulling off to the side of the road so she could get a picture of both of us standing in front of the "Welcome to the Sunshine state" sign. She must have take a dozen pictures so she could just get the perfect picture. They all looked the same to me no matter angle she took them from. Feeling completely drained we entered the nearest Burger Kind we could find and took advantage of the value menu in every way we could. Hoping to God that this fast food venture wouldn't end up like the one in San Diego with Leah, something finally went as planned.

Patricia and I checked in to the Holiday Inn and proceeded to unload all of our belongings while smoking a few joints before we went off to our first game. Patricia explained in great detail that smoking weed wasn't cheating; it was just a nice little relaxed. Not having an addiction problem and seeing how marijuana wasn't addictive, I partake in her actions.

Walking hand in hand to her first baseball game, we get there in the bottom of the second inning to watch the Cincinnati Reds and the New York Yankees. Being a long time hatter of any New York team, I viciously root for the Cincinnati Reds and give a standing ovation to Brandon Phillips and Joey Votto every time they get up to the plate. Patricia is constantly telling me to calm down as she has a big smile across her face. My eyes find their way over to her as she is sitting down, she is wearing an old fashioned white dress that shows her freshly shaven legs plus a jean jacket on and her sunglasses sitting perfectly on top of her head. I wonder to myself if it is okay to love her and possibly try to be with her, but somehow I know that it will end up wrong.

By the end of the game, she is just excited and into it as I am while sitting on my lap watching as the team I want to win for once does. Grabbing a couple hot dogs on our way out, we spend the rest of the night strolling through town making fun of anything and everything we can find. I ask her how school is going and without looking at me she says that her and her mom decided it was best to get home schooled. Not wanting her to think that I believe there was anything wrong with that, I tell her she is lucky she doesn't have to wake up early and deal with all the bullshit school brings. Smiling innocently at me, Patricia tells me that she knows the I try too hard to say the right thing all the time and that it leaves me constantly questioning everything in life. I can't argue the girl is right about everything she says to me. Patricia asks me if I still lie in bed and think about my future all the time and let myself get lost in my own scheme of thoughts. I tell her that not much has changed with me. She glances another look at me, this time asking me if I have yet to buy myself an iPod. Once again I tell her no, explaining that college has robbed me of every dime I have. It's a shame you have to pay all of that back and you don't even have a degree, she whispers to me. Before she stops taking jabs at me, Patricia says how lame it is that the newest band I listen to is the Black Crowe's first album. The worse part in all of this is she is right about everything. Our walk started out hand in hand and now has left me walking with my hands in my pocket.

We have two days left before we pack up again and head home and I spend it mostly by myself watching Cincinnati Reds games and eating as many hot dogs I can while using my still useful fake i.d. to drink as many beers as my stomach will allow. The hotel feels lonely and I hate waking up in places that aren't my home. I'm feeling guilty about dropping out of college and how I make it in this big bad world. I also wonder how my actions have affected my parents and their mental stability. Being their only son, they invested a lot of time and mental health on me and I don't know if I can make them proud anymore. Once in my life I was this nice kid that dated one girl and never got fucked up on alcohol, weed, the occasional cocaine, and prescription meds.

Patricia spends the rest of her stay in the sunshine state buying clothes and working on her Hollywood look. She wakes up early every morning and makes me peanut butter and jelly sandwiches while telling teasing me about being a man stuck in a child's body. I never put up much of a fight because once again she is right about everything. Her morning breath is a little on the unpleasant side but her hair and lips always look really sexy. Patricia and I have yet to have sex on this trip and I know it is the first thing on both of our minds.

The last morning there we sit on the edge of the bed and talk about our dreams. She tells me she plans on moving out to California to be an actress, to make this happens and how much she would love to prove everyone who made fun of her growing up regret it. Putting a smile on my face I tell her not to take everything to heart and that people often times only say things to you that they think about themselves. Not wanting to go any deeper into the subject she asks me what my plans are now. Placing my hand on her knee, she jerks just a little before allowing me to keep it there. I tell her that I plan on moving to New York and possibly being a big time movie producer. Patricia tells me that it sounds like a fun idea and that she believes I could pull it off.

Tired of talking I finally do what both of us had been thinking about and take her by the hand and we start-making love just once more. For the first time in my life it is romantic. Going at it slowly she keeps looking into my eyes and it disturbs me at first but eventually I just go along with it. Her moans are quick and have a crying sound to them. This is nothing like I have ever done and it feels pleasant and awkward at the same time.

We pack up our things and head home. The drive feels like a much quicker one than before and she spends the drive staring out the window as I let her have the radio station of her choice. Patricia and I rarely talk and when we do it is a trivial thing. Once again mocking me about my taste in music she quotes The Black Crowes song She Talks to Angels.

She never mentions the words addiction
In certain company
Yea she'll tell you she's an orphan
After you meet her family

I think Patricia looks at herself as being the girl in the song she loves it. I can tell by the look in her eyes.

I drop her off at her home and this time while getting out she lets me know that she won't be seeing me anymore and that this time it is truly the end. Getting dump doesn't feel so good, does it? Patricia also mentions that the baby is Stan's, then she turns and says or maybe it's my aunts or just maybe it is yours. I just drive off feeling like a total asshole and take it as another brick in the wall.

Upon returning home, I decided that I was going to visit James gravesite. Everyday for the next six months I would stop by his gravesite and talk to it. I knew that I wasn't really talking to James and that he couldn't hear me but it felt good to do it anyway. Telling him everything that was going on in my life and how things have changed. Somewhere inside of me I hoped that he could hear me. Maybe he is in a place where he doesn't hurt anymore. Maybe that peace that he searched so hard for on earth he finally found. Perhaps, there is even a heaven and a God.

His death made me more focused on life. I didn't

want to breakdown for good and waste away. That would have made things much more badly. Picking myself from off the ground and trying to succeed was what I had to do. James wouldn't have wanted me to throw my life away. The only way I could make good with what had happened was to march forward in life and become the best me that I could be. I couldn't imagine a world without James in it. It was weird not having someone you were so close to not being there anymore. I decided to leave his phone number in my contacts list. As silly as it may be this made me feel like he was still here in a way.

It was the only thing that was left to connect me to him. So many times I would call his cell phone just to hear his voice mail. This made me cry every time because it was a quick reminder of what I had missed. After awhile I stopped crying when I heard it and I started to smile. The reason I started to smile was because it was something that I could keep and it was never too far away from me. I knew his passing would take a long time to heal from.

Because we never get over a death. Losing someone you love takes something out of your heart that won't come back. But I started to believe that when that part in your heart is gone, God replaces it with understanding and undying love. That will last a lifetime. His touch will start to hide those scars that you earned so much.

The time had come that I had to stay at home. With everything that had happened sitting home was sort of refreshing. The things that were on my mind came down to one. And that was Dani. She was the only one at that school who gave a damn about me. Dani was the only person that I met there that wasn't fake. She was real in every sense of the word. Her difficulties in life were something she overcame and they made her a strong person instead of someone who is afraid of life.

Dani would send me pictures through her phone of the

fun she was having throughout summer. Those pictures were the only things I looked forward to getting. My comments were always juvenile. Telling her how hot she looked and how much I missed her. She was on my mind twenty four/ seven. Dani and I started to make plans about meeting up and doing something.

I found that the attention I got from her was the only thing keeping me from going insane this time. She was someone who made me a better person and hope that maybe life wasn't as dreary as I constantly made it out to be. Unfortunately, my spin on everything consisted of something that was negative and sarcastic. But that is only because I call it as I see it. Still though, I was having trouble finding something superficial about her.

Have you ever seen someone who made you rethink everything you know? And when you see them it just makes you feel different about everything that has happened before. Sort of like all the scars, bumps, and bruises that life has given just faded away. That is how I felt with each passing day about Dani. When she came to my college it was as though there was finally something lifted off of me. I couldn't describe it really except that I had never felt anything like that before.

She was beautiful and everyone paid attention to her. I felt so nervous every time that I saw her. Getting the nerve worked up just to speak to her seems like an impossible task. The words just wouldn't come and I was always left just looking down whenever I passed her in the hallway. What would she think if she knew about my past and me? My year had previously been a scary one not one that you want to talk about and ever bring up with a girl that you want to impress.

I started thinking of the first time that I ever saw her and how she made me feel. She was the girl I never imagined being able to have. With everything that was going on with me back during the school year I started to forget just what an impact she made on me.

Dani was in three of my classes and at the end of our English class the bell rang and like in every school every student grabs their belongings and sprints for the door. On the way out I ran right into her. She dropped all of her books and when everything hit the floor it just went all over. I quickly started saying my apologies and scattering all over the floor to pick her books up. Very strangely, she just looked at me as though I was completely ridiculous and she was probably right. Dani didn't speak one word to me. I felt so embarrass. How could I have been so damn stupid? An opportunity comes along and what do I do? Completely fuck it up. I run into her spilling her books everywhere and the only thing I can come up with is a very soft spoken stuttering I'm a I'm a sorry. Man there goes that opportunity.

I spent the next couple of weeks now thinking about her more and more than ever before. No matter what I would do I would think about her and damn I just couldn't get her out of my mind. You know how sometimes you just can't fall asleep because there is so much on your mind. You lay there thinking and thinking about everything. Your day, how it went, what tomorrow will be like. And if you lay there long enough thinking you will for sure lose your mind like you never thought you could. I thought to myself night in and night out "Should I say something to her again"? Should I take that chance and be completely humiliated again?

All of that awkwardness didn't matter anymore. Dani and I never imagined things turning out the way they did. I wasn't upset that things were happening like this either.

As the summer went along I slowly but steadily pulled myself back together again. Often times I wondered if Stan had played a part in any of this. The hatred I had for that fucker was out of control. Up until that point in my life I never truly wanted anything bad to happen to anyone but he changed that. The damage he had caused was mind blowing. From Patricia's slow descent into hell from James losing control and eventually killing himself. Stan had a hand in all of this and I blamed him whole-heartedly for everything. Wanting so bad to track him down and make him pay for everything I just found myself becoming a hardening person. This wasn't healthy the least bit. All's it did was hurt me. So what was the point anymore?

In life you waste a lot of time waiting for someone to get what is coming to him or her. The truth is we all eventually get what's coming to us. We all do things in our lifetime that are wrong and repercussions are usually followed. But when would Stan finally get what was coming to him? He needed a rude of awakening and severs punishment handed to him.

I spent so much time thinking about killing Stan. I wanted him dead. There were so many nights I lay awake plotting of ways to kill him. Not only did I want him to die, but also I wanted him to suffer a pain and agonizing death. The plans of killing him were well constructed in my head.

Today I bought a gun. It felt so nice. I went to the shooting range and fired four rounds. Every shot I took was dead on. I found pleasure and relaxation in doing this. Something about it felt natural as though I should have had this all along.

What would it look and feel like to kill an individual? To see the last moments of life in their eyes and watch as you decide their fate. To see their blood spill all over the floor and see how much blood they had in them. Seeing how the blood is so red that it looks black.

Why continue to lead an honest life when you can easily turn around and get fucked for it. Sometimes doing the right thing means swallowing all that you believe in and hoped to be true in the world. Taking the wrong side and being the problem sometimes is the only way to cure your hunger for justice. The world is never going to give you justice. So why not take matters into your own hands? I wanted to stop letting everyone else's decisions dictate my life. The control I once felt over my life was now no more. It was completely drained from me in every possible way, shape, and form. I just wanted to start taking matters into my own hands and solving my own problems and not worrying about the consequences that would follow.

Life just has a way of getting you when you least expect it. When you think all is finally fine and dandy, something comes along and changes your outlook on everything. But sometimes changes happen that make you happy. They have a way of evening out the score. That finally happened.

It was close to the fourth of July and the headline on the paper was one that put a smile on my face. Maybe it shouldn't have but it did. The headline was sad and a tragedy but to me it was something I had wanted to happen for quite sometime. And that was Stan was murdered.

He wasn't suppose to be killed, he was suppose to be busted on drug trafficking charges but things got out of hand and it led to him being stabbed several times until he was dead.

Apparently, the cops made a deal with him that included busting all the people he was in cohorts' with and putting all of them away for a long time. When the planned failed and the men on the receiving end of the drugs knew it, they grabbed Stan. These guys knew that they weren't getting out of it and Stan was behind everything. In the only way they could get even or the closest they could get meant killing Stan. With his arm around Stan's neck the drug dealer shoved a knife in his back several times until when he let go Stan dropped to the ground dead. There he laid face down in the street lifeless. It's ashame when a human gets to the point of Stan. What is even more troubling is when you see a case like this and you feel nothing. And nothing is what I felt.

Ballad of Life and Death

Innocent in a minute
Trial by fire in an hour
These words are hard to come by
And these feelings kept inside
Memories are a dime a dozen
And these clouds are timeless rain
Do we desire love or endless heartache?
Wishing well but living the hand dealt
It's sweet yet bitter, hoping sunshine
While praying for the seduced
I'm a virgin, but I whore the mind
With thoughts crude and true love blind
And you'll masturbate your time
But my heart is deep and fine
Fire is a man's dependence
Satan's breathe and desire
For destruction and its dire
Need for sanity and life
And our dove flies and dies
By the flame and fingertips of hell
Set the soul and body free
Calm the heart and allow the blind to see
In this together are we
Love the youth

For it's a photograph of our former self

The death of Stan brought another chapter to my life
to a close. Though I wanted Stan dead, the thought that people
I knew dying was tough to deal with. I never understood
death to a point where it impacted my life. Not ever giving it

much thought now was something I regretted.

What was even more troubling to me was not death but the choices we make on an everyday basis. Our entire life is made up of choices. Some of them good and some of them terrible. We don't realize how one decision can change everything in our lives. A simple hello to a stranger from a walking to work instead of driving to not leaving your house. It all affects your daily life. Our decisions are a domino effect on everything. Every decision I started making from the past year was leading me further and further away from whom I really was.

I didn't know what I had become. My life went from your average kid to a college drop out getting over an underage girl to grieving a close death everyday to falling in love again to wanting to kill people. The leaps were large but now positive. When I talked to people from my home it was as though I never knew the guy I once was.

It was a struggle to fake that I was in front of my family. Not only did I do a terrible job at trying to be who I once was but also no one knew who I had become. When my father looked at me it was as though he could see right through me. How couldn't he? He was my father and someone that raised me my whole entire life. He knew when something was wrong with me. The look in his eyes was sad.

My father knew that he no longer could connect with his own flesh and blood. He tried all the time but I blocked every attempt he made. With all that had occurred, I lost any desire to connect with anyone. I just wanted to be on my way and find out who I really was. Nothing that had previously mattered to me just a year ago meant anything anymore. I wasn't concerned with money and a good education. No longer was I concerned with finding the love of my life or getting a good lay from time to time

The isolation I put myself in became the only thing I knew. It didn't make me depressed either, it made me content.

Every time that I had to interact with people I dreaded the thought. Slowly, it became harder and harder for me to wake up out of this phase. Maybe it wasn't a phase; maybe this is who I truly was.

To make my mother happy, I always told her that I was doing fine and just exploring my options in the world. Hurting my mother was something I had no intention on doing. She rested all of her happiness on the shoulders of my attitude. If I was sad, she was sad, if I was happy, she was happy. So I did what any son who cared about his mother would do and that was fake happiness and content.

Maybe I was good at faking my emotions and maybe I wasn't. Either way they believed it or a more realistic approach is they didn't want to rock the boat and that was fine with me.

My dreams became more and more vivid. They were the only things that I held onto. It was the only thing that linked me to my past. As I drifted off to sleep the magic happened again.

It was the summer of 1999 and school had just let out for the final time in third grade. As I was getting off the bus it I felt like a huge weight was lifted off of my shoulders. For the next three months there would be no waking up early, tests, and school lunches. There was something about the last day of school that every kid found magical. The feeling of freedom being so near was not something that could be understood by anyone that wasn't a current student. It was a time of joy.

Running up to my house, my parents were doing yard work and I went about my business. Jumping on my bicycle I rode throughout the neighborhood and sang my favorite songs. The air was so easy to breathe in and it was as though this is how life should always be. Life didn't get any better or innocent than this.

This time when I woke up, I was greeted by a text

message from Dani. She was going to stop by and see me. I couldn't remember the last time I felt that happy. Trying to look the best I could, I took me a little over than a half hour to get ready.

We met up at the local mall and we decided to see a movie together. The movie was five hundred days of summer. The plot and moral behind the movie was funny to me. I should have taken its advice when it came to Patricia and every other girl that I ever got involved in. Dani enjoyed the movie and we spent the rest of the day walking around the mall and making fun of the movie. She had a way of putting a smile on my face when everything seemed hopeless. She was this breath of fresh air that could cure any feeling and emotion you were struggling with. Dani's smile was also something to take notice of. Her teeth were perfectly straight and white.

Walking around I got the feeling she wanted me to hold her hand and that is what I did. It was the only time I ever held a girls hand and wanted to. Doing so, didn't feel like an obligation but instead nice. The only time I felt that things were getting better for me was when she came around. Which made me wonder just how deep my issues really were? Was I really that bad off? Did I just craze female companionship? Whatever the case was, I felt good to be in her presence.

Dani did everything she could not to bring up the coming school year. Knowing the impact the conversation might have one me. I respected this but it didn't matter anymore if I talked about it or if I just ignored it. She mentioned that she and Mia were patching up their friendship and they might be roommates again. This got my attention quite quickly. It made me feel very uneasy. Once again the questions arose, did Dani know of my night with Mia? Did Dani know everything that Mia had told me?

The way girls constantly talk with each other and

other so-called friends it wouldn't surprise me if she knew everything. Actually, it would have shocked me to know that Dani didn't know of anything. If she did she hid it very well around me. I was starting to get the feeling that Dani might like me a little more than just a friend. She never had a boyfriend and her experiences with guys were limited so if she was trying to get close to me that meant she wanted to be my girlfriend. Right? This was something I was hoping for a lot. The positive effect she would have on my life could turn everything around for me.

Finally holding her hand we decided to grab some ice cream and just talk about our summers. Dani had explained all the fun she was having, going on mission trips with her church and spending quality family time. Was there anything wrong with this girl? I mean she had it rough with all the expectations and pressure and she shone through it becoming a better person. This gave me hope that maybe there was still a chance for me to be happy and content.

When it came time for me to speak about my summer I just lied right through my teeth. What was I going to tell her? That I laid awake at night thinking about killing people? That I had no idea who I was or had finally become. My lies consisted around me telling her that I was having fun exploring the state and just relaxing. I also managed to tell her that I was going back to college. This made her real excited, which led to her giving me a nice friendly hug. I felt bad for lying to her, but a girl like this wasn't going to stick around with a guy who was a drop out and had no real future plans.

She would find out soon enough of my current lie. It wasn't an issue for me to consider just yet.

I drove her back to her car and told her what a great time I had with her. She quickly leaned in a kissed me. Before I could give an honest response Dani hoped into her vehicle and took off. Even though I couldn't tell her how I was feeling, the moment was nice and that's how I wanted to remember it.

Don't know that I will but until I can find me
A girl that'll stay and won't play games behind me
-Neil Diamond-

Never To Fade Away

There you are chasing the clouds away
Live for tomorrow, I'll be here today
No distance too far
There is no mile
Heavens innocence in your smile
Lighting up the nighttime sky
Soaring through the wind
Like a bird spreading its wings to fly

If heaven were a minute
You'd be the day
Sleeping with angels
Washing your tears away
When I'm gone, my heart will stay
So don't ever cry
I love you more than words can say

Kiss the years
They run so fast
Our memories
Are just photographs
From our past
That seem to last
Never to fade away

Holding you forever in my arms
There are no worries
There are no harms
Moments are just a timeless race
Weaving in n out a timeless space
Eyes of gold tender face

Kiss the years
They run so fast
Our memories
Are just photographs
From our past
That seem to last
Never to fade away
South Side of Sanity

Chapter 10
It's A Great Life

The human mind is an ever so changing thing in life. It is one of those crucial things in life that people think is a constant, but in reality it is anything but. Our mind is constantly changing and there is nothing we can do about it, we are helpless and hopeless in trying to do so.

I guess what was the more troubling obstacle for me was that my mind had changed rapidly. I didn't know how to slow it down and was starting to develop a fear that it would never get back to where I needed it. Night after night I would lay awake in my bed and try to recapture what I thought I had lost for good. If I could go back to those nights I would tell myself that what I thought I was losing was in reality something I was gaining from experience. We try so hard to hold onto our past that we forget there is a present and future to take care of. The past doesn't mean anything because you can't do anything to alter it. It is as final as one could hope to accomplish. However, the present and future are in our hands of fate.

We have all of the necessary tools to make it good yet we find ourselves drowning in a pool of past regrets and unfulfilled promises. One of my biggest flaws in life was being able to give productive advice that I couldn't seem to take and follow. I always thought to myself if I had someone else's life I could make it perfect in a matter of days. If I knew the amount of times I stepped back in what I was doing and just thought to myself this couldn't be my life. This couldn't be who I was. I would have gone insane years earlier.

The realization finally came to me that this didn't

have to be my life; this isn't how life had to be. It is all about choice. And my choice was now to turn it around. With everything that happened it was as though life was flying by me. I guess it was true what everyone had told me, the older you get the faster the years go. I kept looking at my phone a starring at Dani's number. If I could have just thought through my decisions I could've been back at the university holding her in my arms. But the thought of staying there after everything was too much.

I don't think I could've done it. Everything about that place left a bad taste in my mouth and no matter what I did it wouldn't come out. The air in that town, the setup of the town, and even the homework in the classes were too old. Still, all's it took was one girl to make you miss something no matter how terrible things were at the time. And Dani was that girl.

I made the tough decision to return home for the fall semester and get a job in hopes of making some money to get out of the one horse town. That job came for me and it consisted of flipping burgers at the McDonalds' near my house. Everyday I woke up and got ready to go to a job that I despised more than staying at the university. It didn't help that I had let myself fall in love again. Why do I consistently keep doing this to myself I often wondered.

Not thinking of how embarrassing it might be driving back to my former college, I hopped into my old beat up car and drove there. During that ride I listened to my favorite John Mellencamp's disc Rain on the Scarecrow and headed down that highway thinking that all of my problems were going to be filled. Even if all of my problems would be filled all the holes in my head would be larger. That dreadful drive finally came to an end as I climb out of that car and decided to smoke a cigarette. The air was bitterly cold and the wind only added to my current frustration. Feeling like a kid in junior high I tried to gather the courage to call Dani and tell her I decided to give her a surprise visit from a caring friend. But instead I thought it would be a better surprise to wait for her by her dorm.

It felt like hours went by when in reality it was just over a half hour until I saw Mia and one of Dani's friends. The only thing that crossed my mind at that point was fuck I have to deal with another useless conversation with this psycho bitch. What they had in store for me was something I knew they had waited forever to do, and that was tell me how much Dani doesn't ever want to see me again on the account of my one piss poor judgment night with Mia. Standing feeling like a complete loser I just left. Why the hell would I just leave without trying to explain things to Dani? There was an honest explanation for what had happened that night and truthfully my head wasn't fastened tight at the moment. It was as though another nail had been driven into the coffin.

The reason I didn't want to stay and talk things out with the girl I spent all day and night thinking about was because I knew she deserved better than what I could offer her. In many ways I did the first smart thing in my life because I didn't hang around to pull an innocent girl capable of great things down my lonesome screwed up life. The love and care I had for her didn't allow me to wreck her. It just wasn't the right thing to do and even though I had told myself several times that I'd let her go and let things be I never could just let go. How a girl I never had sex with mean so much to my life? I felt so in touch and attached to her. All the sexual experiences and mistakes with women who clouded my life never meant what this meant to me. Even Patricia didn't do this to me. And that was something I was grateful for. My relationship with Patricia led me down roads no one wants to go down and our whole connection was based on sexual frustration. That's never a solid ground to base anything positive on.

Dani wasn't like her or the rest; she was what I spent

my whole life waiting for. All the same I had to walk away. Once again the drive home like so many before began and ended with disappointment.

Getting back home I did what I had done my whole life and that was lying on my bed plotting my next move in what I called a life. Those thoughts led me where I was hiding since James had passed away and that was an endless tear. The tears were warm and hard. It felt like they each weighed a thousand pounds on my post puberty face. He was gone and the fact that he was actually gone had finally began to settle in. To know someone and call them friend and have them mean something to you is special. That's what my father had always told me. Friends are more special than family a lot of times. You are with family and become one because God threw you together and it's not a choice that you are related to. It's only natural to love family because you know you are supposed to but a friend in something really special and unique. If someone is your friend it is because they choose to be; someone out there likes you for whom you are and enjoys spending time with you because you make them happy. That is the ultimate gift in life. Someone else enjoying you is the most loving thing God ever created.

Losing James was much more than just losing a friend it was losing a person who thought I was worth their precious time on earth. Through all of my heartache I always made it because there were people who just appreciated my very existence. I know it doesn't sound like a big deal to some because some have everything life has to offer and they take it for granted every step of the way, but for me it meant everything. It meant having a reason to get out of my bed in the morning and continue on when everything else seemed so bleak and wrong.

I continued my visits to James grave and continued my usual talks with the tombstone. At night sometimes I'd stay up there and talk to it; people think its scary and strange to do that but I always felt it was more personal and real doing it that way. For some reason I felt like he was actually there when I spoke.

Though all of that was hard to leave behind me, I knew it was the best thing to do. Finally I erased his number and stopped leaving messages on his phone. For some unknown reason God let it play out. It is hard to understand people as humans when they speak so harsh about individual's souls when they commit suicide. They always tell of how God won't let that person in heaven and that it is written in clear black and white in the bible. I believe the bible is full of shit a lot of times. Actually, if some of its full of shit then the whole thing must be. Right? What makes a person believe that God will damn someone for that? No one wants to end their life, no one wants everything to come crashing down on them and completely lose their mind and sanity. God is with someone at all times, even when they are about to take their own lives.

God knows people on a level that people don't know themselves on and he knows when a troubled soul has had enough and can't make it. That's not to say people should do that when times get tough because life is tough and love is war. God is the only who knows when its time for someone to come home. Believe it or not he sometimes won't answer your prayers. God isn't always going to be there for you; sometimes you need to be there for yourself. One thing is for sure though he is always listening.

Time had continued to go slow in that room so I thought it appropriate to look through all of my yearbooks and photos when I was young. Or should I say younger. Dazing into those books and photos I had realized just how good things actually were for me. I had spent so much time living in the negative that I forgot how to function in the positive. Standing on my feet I went over to the mirror and saw the loneliness in my eyes and heart. I had allowed myself to become hollow and stop working on a healthy level. What had I become I thought to myself? Too young for this discontentment and life.

My past had awakened me inside and gave me another shot at making it work. I thought to myself to move forward in life I had to resolve the past first because every time that I had tried to make it work in the present I found myself being paralyzed in the past. It was like a cycle that didn't stop until I could finally say I had enough. Actually, it was more like feeling I had enough.

No one truly knows what it's like to lose everything until they're alone. The loneliness wasn't the problem I often said it was the fact that it was I that was spending the time alone. If I were someone else I wouldn't mind being alone because the time would be treasured instead of dreaded. Dreaded like a homeless person dreads a blizzard.

Today was a different kind of feeling, it was one that brought ease and hope to my world. Hitting rock bottom was like a dream come true in a sick demented way. It showed that everything else couldn't get any worse it could only bring me up. Even if it meant just a damn little bit, it still was a step in the right direction.

Gathering all of my money that day which consisted of six dollars and twenty cents I headed downtown and waited for my shift to start. Smoking a cigarette in the back of the fast food future I watched as all the people walked in an out of that fucking place. The place was a walking heart attack and people indulged themselves in every dollar sandwich that they could fit in their weekly budget. I was never the type to judge people a little more than a year ago but now since I was a miserable fuck I might as well dislike everyone as much as I disliked myself. My boss came outside to let me know that I had to get my ass in there and start serving America's fat assess. Waiting by the drive thru window I spent the next eight hours putting up with everyone's bullshit. You know your day isn't going well when a four hundred pound fat fuck bitches you out because his daughter already has the toy inside the happy meal and it's your fault when the joint is out of the one toy she wanted. It was times like these that I wish I had robbed a poor little lady for money.

Finally the workday had come to a close and I was exhausted from the daily encouragement from the boss and the helpful coworkers. After receiving my paycheck I headed down to the local liquor store and bought the cheapest bottle of liquor I could find. I believe Night Train was the name of the poison that night. Calling up the friends that I had a while ago went to the strip club with we headed back to my place and drank ourselves in oblivion.

To make our drink more sensible we blasted Guns N Roses Appetite for Destruction through my stereo and really turned up the song Night Train to commemorate the occasion. I drank more alcohol in that night than I had in my short but eventful stay in college. This time I wasn't fortunate enough to get laid by a Dassel in distress. Instead my friends and I stayed up and bullshitted the night away. I told them of my plan to get the fuck out of that town and see the world but I knew my words were nothing but a dream from a drunken kid who didn't have a bucket to piss in.

The morning that followed was one that left me with a hangover and late for a job that almost took a resume for me to get. It took every little bit of strength I had to get myself off of that couch and get ready to go to work again. My body ached and my head felt like it weighed a hundred pounds plus somewhere along the night I must have hurt my ribs pretty badly because they felt like someone had beaten me with a baseball bat. I didn't question the pain because knowing myself which at times I'm pretty sure I didn't I probably deserved it.

When I arrived to work my boss told me that this was the last straw and that I was fired. It didn't surprise me the least bit and actually I felt quite relieved that I didn't have to go back there and deal with people. This was an ongoing issue I saw evolving in my life. Every damn job that I got I managed to fuck up and that went along with school also. I was coming to the conclusion that I was just a total and complete fuck up. I couldn't even hold down a part time job standing by a damn window asking someone if they wanted large or small fries. But why should've that surprised me? That was just the way everything had gone for me. Here at one moment and a memory the next. At least I had the pleasure for a short period of time even if the memories sucked too.

Not having the balls to tell my father that I had once again lost another job I decided to just walk around town until what would have been my shift was over. The weather once again was turning from fall to winter and that feeling of the holidays was setting in. I always found myself being the Charlie Brown type whenever the holidays came rolling around. There was just something about the time that made me feel like life was all-materialistic and just another reason to buy senseless shit that no one really needed.

The real reason the holidays left me feeling the way I did was because I constantly spent it without the girl that always decided to pop in an out of my life. This time around I wanted to try to get my family some of that senseless shit that no one actually wanted. My bank account was a laughing matter but I managed to keep four hundred dollars in there. That was a hope that quickly turned away when I had to pay off a fine that I managed to keep away until the cops put me in the county jail for a weekend and that still didn't pay it off.

I had kept just enough money to send a letter off to Dani in hopes of not getting her back but possibly to understand. To understand that I never planned to hurt her or myself and that in life sometimes shit just fucking happens.

At first I was going to send out an email but that seemed too much of a rushed effort. Sending a text seemed like the drunken thing to do and calling her seemed like the creep thing to do. Also I wanted her to imagine me sitting down and putting all of my thoughts and efforts into this. My ink on the paper would be last thing she knew was hers sent from me.

I found it awkward an unfortunate turn of events that I was the one writing the letter this time instead of receiving one from Patricia. At least my letter wasn't to inform her that I was pregnant.

Dear Dani,

Where would I start writing this letter to you? I don't quite know how to tell you certain things because it just seems too fragile to bring up. I thought to myself that I could never get this hooked on a girl without having sex with her and then all of sudden you came along and turned my heart inside out. I figured that all of the useless empty one-night stands made me into a man and that I was fulfilled with that. The truth being told, I was never the guy who wanted to be a part of that scene and stereotype. I did it to make sense of this fucked up thing I call a life. The walk home with you during that first semester did something to me that no one has had the ability to do. It made me want to stop waking up alone and pretending that it was ok to not feel others presence in their lives. You're right to not want to take a leap of faith on me; you're right to not want to be a part of my plans. I would break your heart and leave you with a much bitter taste for men than what we really deserve. Believe it or not that wouldn't be my fault because everything I do is not intentional but somehow hurts those around me. I just want you to understand and feel that I never wanted to hurt you. It was never in my thoughts to let you down. I hope you find what you're looking for because if anyone deserves it, it's

182

you.

Never yours …

Sending that letter off gave me a sense of accomplishment that I hadn't felt in quite sometime. In fact, it changed my thoughts and me on this cycle of breath we all take. For once I actually moved on in life and put that part to rest. I even ended my constant rage for everyone on this earth. The world is a big bad place that screws us all over and somehow I was fine with all of that. All of the shit and complications now seemed like a simple roadblock to get where I needed to be.

Christmas finally came and with it brought a nice snowfall that gave a certain peace in my heart and mind. I managed to grab my last paycheck at my job and I used it to supply gifts for my parents and family. It was nice for once to give my sister something on a special occasion than my usual case of bullshit of why I couldn't get her something.

It's funny how we think we can fool our parents so easily and that they didn't have a clue as to what eats away at us on a constant level. My father sat me down to let me know that he could see the obvious heartache that I was carrying around for more than a year. While the talk was hard to do at first it showed that we weren't as different as I had previously thought. He was a lot like me in certain ways and didn't want me to fall any deeper in discontentment than I already had. He looked at me and handed me a check that would take care of tuition to the school I spent dreaming about since late junior high.

It was my ticket to get out of the boring Midwest town that I had dreaded my entire life and a chance to see New York City and attend the film school. For years I would think about being the next Stephen Spielberg but settled on a local college to pursue a degree in psychology. Perhaps I decided back then to go after that degree in hopes of figuring out what was wrong with me. I apparently didn't stick around long enough to find out.

I spent the rest of my Christmas with my family sitting around and talking like we did when I was younger and it felt like that was the way it should've always been. Sitting there I took in all of what was going on because I knew I would be leaving within the next few weeks and that these moments would end up being few and far between. Not only that but my heart felt like it could beat again without all of that constant trouble that seemed to plague it for way too damn long.

The next few weeks got here in a blink of an eye an all of sudden I was almost on my way to the big apple. This time when I packed to head to school I didn't take everything that I have ever owned and dwell on it the whole time I was gone. It was time for a change and a change is what was coming. Packing as few things as I possibly could, I didn't pack photos, those old yearbooks, or anything with sentimental value to it because it risked bringing me to where I didn't want to be.

In my time since high school I felt I did everything that I needed to in this old town and needed to get out and experience what God had created for all of us to see. I had allowed myself to get suffocated with all of the mixed up people and lays that surround our everyday lives. I grew up and went insane a million times since entering that university and leaving it. Not only did I leave it but also I left behind a part of my life that had meant something to me. No matter how much I may have disliked it at the time.

Taking one more spin through town before I headed out for a long while I stopped to get gas and ran into Patricia as I was done paying for the gas and we both looked at each other with initial shock but all's we manage to say to one another was hello. I guess in a way that was nice instead of stopping and having a conversation that made us both feel awkward.

Patricia actually seemed like she matured mentally as I watched her leave that gas station. Perhaps, in another lifetime we could have been together and made things work. After all, she was potentially the mother of my child and someone who I found myself relating to a lot since our last breakup.

I never thought it would take the amount of time it did to get over Patricia, I guess in a big way we never really get over someone that had such a large impact on our lives. Her hair had changed to a beach blonde style to which I hated. Why the hell do women think that being blonde is better looking? My experiences in life have shown me that blondes are much less fun in bed. For the most part they have just lain there and didn't care how or when they got fucked, just as long as they did. Brunettes on the other hand, desired more than the tedious sex that was most common.

Upon leaving, I noticed there was no car seat in the back, hopefully that meant she wasn't pregnant after all. Regardless, it had been over with finally.

I have always found it quite strange how someone that used to mean so much to you can turn into a stranger in a matter of months. She uses to be closer to me than anyone but somehow through all of everything that we call life we both got lost in the turmoil of being young. There was a time when after seeing her I would have stopped and spent the next week thinking about and debating whether or not I want to give her a call but now things were different and I was on my way to something new.

Sometimes God has a way of throwing a few things at you at once. As I got into my vehicle I looked down at my phone and saw that Dani had sent me a text message. The text message stunned me at first because it read good luck I'm positive you will be making some memorable films real soon. She also put a smiley face at the end of the message so

I think that means it was legitimate.

Almost dying to know how she knew what I was doing I had a feeling someone close to me gave her the tip. I thought it in bad taste to ask her or anyone for that matter to keep me from looking desperate. Regardless, I was happier than a pig in shit that she decided to get a hold of me and give me that bit of information. I assumed she got my letter and did indeed forgive me. It was as though all of those months spent praying had started to prove fruitful for me. Because all of the things that found its way into my life and plagued it were resolving themselves and coming out just a little better than when I went into those situations.

Cruising down the road I let all the windows open and had Kiss Alive blaring through the stereo. It actually felt like I was at the concert. I enjoyed everything that was going on around me. All the Americans in their vehicles with shitty music on and their middle fingers in the air made me feel right at home. I watched closely as the sun was glaring off of everything and the skies were as blue beyond beautiful.

All of that deep thought and stress that I put into everything was vanishing quickly and now was replaced with joy for a different and new start. For all the time that I spent wanting to burn down the world and all of its fake wrong doing people I was now happy to be a part of everything. I didn't care any more about the trivial things in life that clouded everything and made life so complicated and rough. Life is too short to live in pain and regret.

We as humans are made with so many emotions that we just don't know how to deal with all of them and find ourselves turning to harmful ideas to ruin our ability to feel. Society doesn't know how to feel anymore. It's tough to make it anymore and be capable of anything but destruction because it's all that we know.

I found myself stuck in the same old ways and hurtful mind frame because I was just that, stuck. When you are stuck and you don't know the logical way of getting out you tend to spin your tires in the mud and make matters in life even tougher to deal with.

Whether you believe in a Christian God, Buddha, or Indian spirit the important thing is that you believe in something bigger than you that will pull you through when you least expect it. Something that in times of sorrow and need will provide comfort and you don't know why it does but it just does. Life isn't meant to be analyzed and beaten to death. People do that too often and find themselves cold and bitter way too damn long. It's all made up of faith, everything comes down to one's faith to make through life alive.

Arriving into the city was a blessing in disguise for me, the lights lit up the nighttime sky and the traffic that crowded one street held more vehicles than my entire town. I thought of it as a first priority to check out 42nd street and get a taste of what life was like in the big time. Seeing that was a major culture shock and it left me dazed for days. The sight of everyone running around to the next store or bar was unusually warming for me and I thought to myself that this is what life was meant to feel like. I still never understood why that man at the tobacco store was so mean; New York City was filled with life and new and different opportunities. I even enjoyed the polluted air that clogged my lungs.

There are a few things that I have learned through my walk of life and they're this, life is never fair, love is meant to hurt like hell for awhile but damn the feeling of falling in it is better than anything ever witnessed, and no matter how terrible your life scenario may seem, there is always a way out. Believe it or not, there is a higher power out there just waiting for you to call upon it and truly want to make the difference. I thought to myself if it weren't for hard times I would have no character, personality, or desire to burn the world down on a daily basis or just try to fix it with one damaged soul at a time. Maybe someday I will put this into a book and call it All of Satan's Men. But this side of life was much different than the one I had previously known. Actually this is the South Side of Heaven. Looking up to the sky where I had spent my whole life believing the heavens were I softly said to myself, God it feels good to be alive.

The End.

Bye, bye it's been a sweet love
But this feeling I can't change
Please don't take it so badly
Cause the Lord knows I'm to blame.
-Lynyrd Skynyrd-

Acknowledgments

I would like to dedicate this book to my dad for being the greatest father out there along with being one of the best friends I ever could possibly hope for. Thank you for always being there and being the rock I needed. I wouldn't be who I was today without your love and guidance. And to my mom for giving birth and always letting me be who I am. I love you two more than words can describe.

I'd like also to thank my incredibly sweet and gorgeous niece Molly Mae Hoffman. With hopes you decide to never read my books.

I would like to also dedicate the book in the memory of my grandmother Kay Hoffman and my maternal grandparents Eldon and Nellie Koch. R.I.P. And to Ryan Scott Koch.

Joshua Flowers- thanks for always being a brother and knowing I am genuinely insane while putting up with my constant strange actions and thoughts. Also for never taking all of my threats to the police and having me locked up for good. You are the greatest. Also, thanks to JoAnn Bird for keeping him that way.

Bradley Tucker- one of the best friends and roommates anyone could ask for. This book wouldn't have been completed if not for your encouragement and challenge towards me to actually get it published.
Michael Ray Hoffman Jr.
To all of my Cousins, Aunts, and Uncles- I love you.

And to all the individuals who inspired me to write this book,
thank you for the material.
(To Her)
Her eyes shined like diamonds
The night was young and still
The sighs were soft and quick
Love was made to kill
Like a touch without a feel
Moments in a dream turned surreal
Much to the devil's deal
That flourished in appeal
Like the secrets whispered to conceal

Heaven bares her smile
Much like a long walked mile
Or the days gone out of style
While we lie in sleep
The thoughts run deep
To our souls for keep
Cradling her during her moment of weep
For the intentions have become cheap
To say I love would off her feet sweep

To this I can't describe
What the city sleeps to hide
Cause the truths are weighed down by lies
Descended into sapphire skies
Our love much like the seasons have died
Though I love her more than I can say
The feelings must creep away
For her touch more like poison convey
Meaning absurd and life astray